Brian turned ⟨on the radio⟩ while
Anne sat be⟨side him⟩ listening intently:

". . . Soviet experiment can cut off all the power
in the world. Industry would be useless. The world
would be paralyzed. My studies convince me that
modern civilization is in great danger."

The announcement ended, and Brian turned off
the radio. "He claims the experiment will cause
widespread *irreparable* power failure. There is no
such thing."

Anne smiled. "That's a relief to me," she said and
stood up.

Suddenly, the lights went out. Anne's hand gripped
Brian's arm. He quickly flipped on the radio. Nothing happened. He opened the door to the hallway. The lights were out. He picked up a flashlight. It wouldn't work. Then he looked at Anne.

Her face was white. "Oh, Brian," she said. "I'm
afraid."

AUTHOR'S PROFILE

Christopher Anvil has been writing professionally in the
science fiction field for more than a decade, with a record
of close to a hundred short stories, novelettes and short
novels published in the field's major magazines. Many of
his stories have appeared in the important best-of-the-
year anthologies. THE DAY THE MACHINES STOPPED is
his first full-length novel.

OTHER SIGNIFICANT MONARCH BOOKS

A Science Fiction Novel

THE DAY
THE MACHINES STOPPED

Christopher Anvil

MONARCH BOOKS, INC.

MONARCH
BOOKS
40c

Derby, Connecticut

THE DAY
THE MACHINES STOPPED

A Monarch Books Science Fiction Novel

Published in December, 1964

Copyright © 1964 by Christopher Anvil

Cover Painting by Ralph Brillhart

Monarch Books are published by MONARCH BOOKS, INC., Capital Building, Derby, Connecticut, and represent the work of outstanding novelists and writers of non-fiction especially chosen for their literary merit and reading entertainment.

Printed in the United States of America

Chapter 1

Brian Philips hated fights. He was strong and capable enough, but the experience of his twenty-nine years suggested that justice didn't always win. Often enough, nobody won; both sides were losers. But experience also told him there were times when it was better even to lose than to back down.

Brian braked his car in the company parking lot, shut off the engine, and looked at his watch. 7:25. He was twenty minutes earlier than usual, and that, he thought, ought to be enough. He glanced around. Although the offices and laboratories of Research East didn't start work till 8:00, according to the schedule, in actual fact the parking lot was even now more than a quarter filled.

The big black car of the corporation president, James Cardan, was already in its usual spot near the door, and the window of Cardan's fourth-floor office was lighted against the dimness of the overcast, early-spring morning. Here and there, Brian noted, other offices and labs were lit up, but not the windows of the lab where he worked as a chemist. That probably meant that he'd arrived before his blond assistant, Anne Cermak. He hoped he'd gotten there about the same time as Carl Jackson.

Brian remembered Carl's comment when for a few moments they'd found themselves alone in the lab some days before:

"This is supposed to be an age of sophistication," Carl had said. "Everyone is supposed to be very civilized with everyone else. But I'm going to make an exception. I want Anne. Stay away from her."

For a moment, Brian didn't speak.

Carl said flatly, "Just so you understand."

Brian said, "Maybe I could just say that's up to Anne.

But I've already spent too much time getting run over by people who knew what they wanted."

"Sorry to hear it."

"So I'll make an exception. *I* want Anne. I'm not staying away from her, either here or outside."

They'd been interrupted then. What would have happened if they hadn't been interrupted, Brian didn't know . . .

He slid out of the car, locked it, and crossed the lot toward the building. A very light drizzle was in his face, and the air felt cold and damp. Here it might be warm by noon, but coming in on the short cut through the wooded hills, the snowbanks had still been piled beside the road. Winter hung on despite the fact that tomorrow would be the first day of April.

As he reached the building and walked up the single broad step, he turned sidewise to shove open the outer door. He noted, as he turned, the mud spattered across the front of Cardan's car, and smiled. Cardan believed in saving time. The ruts, potholes and dizzy horseshoe curves of short cuts through the surrounding hill country made no difference to Cardan. Beside his car was another equally mud-spattered, with a small Roman Numeral I bolted to the grille. This, Brian knew, was one of the company's experimental cars, with the gasoline engine taken out and another power plant put in.

He pushed open the building's inner door, felt the steady, steam-heated warmth, crossed to the elevator, pressed a button marked 4, and a few moments later was walking down the hall to his lab.

As he snapped on the lights he was aware of the familiar sense of pleasure that two years of work at Research East had only made more real. He glanced at the soapstone-topped lab benches, with cabinets underneath for apparatus, that ran down two sides of the small room. He noted the chemical balances in their glass cases, the shelves of reagents in bottles and jars, and, at the far end of the room, the two cubicles with their partitions of wavy glass. He went into the right-hand cubicle, fitted out as a small office, and hung up his coat. Beside his desk, in a low bookcase holding chemical texts and handbooks, was a portable transistor radio that incidentally served as a book end. He glanced at his watch. Almost 7:30. He snapped on the radio for the news summary he usually listened to in his car on the way in.

The sound came on loud, and as Brian turned down the volume, he saw near the leg of his desk, beneath the cord from the phone, a pale-blue square of cloth. He picked it up —a girl's small, clean handkerchief with the letter "A" in one corner. He breathed in the pleasant scent and shut his eyes. For a moment it seemed that Anne was right there before him, a blond girl with dark-blue eyes, a straight nose, a firm chin, and a figure disguised but not hidden by the gray lab coat.

The radio announcer finished an ad for a local bank and started to give the news.

There was a quiet knock on the lab door.

Brian turned up the news a little louder and walked to the door. He was reasonably sure who would be there. Carl Jackson was in the habit of dropping in to talk to Anne before Brian, who had farther to drive, got in in the morning.

Brian opened the door. Carl Jackson blinked, then stepped in and shut the door. He glanced around, scowling. "Where's Anne?"

"Not here yet."

The two men looked at each other. Brian could feel the intensity of Carl's gaze as they measured themselves against each other. Brian stood a fraction under six feet. Carl was about six feet two. Brian weighed a little less than a hundred and eighty. Carl, equally muscular and athletic, weighed over a hundred and ninety. In addition, there was something about Carl's light-blue eyes that suggested sudden anger and lightning reflexes. With his close-cropped pale-blond hair, tanned lean face, and powerful build, Carl presented the appearance of a formidable athlete. Brian felt the sense of oppression of a man physically outclassed by his opponent.

The mutual inspection had lasted only a few seconds, but at the end, Brian could feel his own disadvantage, tinged by a brief sadness, because only a few weeks ago, before

7

Anne had arrived on the scene, he and Carl had been almost friends.

Carl broke into his thoughts abruptly. "How old are you, Brian? About thirty?"

"Twenty-nine," said Brian.

"When's your birthday?"

Brian frowned. "In a few months."

"How much do you make?"

Brian now caught the drift of Carl's questions. There was a chill in his voice as he said, "Why do you ask?"

"About five thousand," said Carl. "Isn't it?"

Brian said nothing, not bothering to volunteer the information that Carl's figure was out of date. Cardan had quickly raised Brian's pay to six thousand five hundred, and Brian had no feeling of being cramped on his salary. A few years ago he would have thought himself lucky to earn half as much.

Carl, his eyes slightly narrowed and glowing an electric blue, said, "I make eleven thousand. Twice what you make. I'm twenty-seven, not almost thirty years old. You've got a dead-end job in a dead-end field. I'm in electronics, the fastest growing field there is." He paused for a moment, then said, "Which of us has the most to offer?"

Brian, feeling the pressure of Carl's physical superiority, and the strain of looking unflinchingly into the hard, confident blue eyes, had the feeling of a man cut off and besieged on every side. Carl's manner showed his awareness of what Brian must be going through. But there was a little quirk in Brian's character that Carl wasn't aware of.

Carl went on. "I've been doing some research on you, Brian. I know in detail just what a mess you made of your life till you finally settled down." He looked Brian up and down, still unaware that Brian functioned a little differently than he did himself, and added, "Just forget about Anne. If you're honest, you'll see you aren't good enough." He paused, then added deliberately, "If you've got any guts at all, that is."

And that did it. All through this torrent of abuse Brian had said nothing in his own defense, had made no angry accusations of his own. He had even been able to see a certain one-sided truth and logic in what Carl said. He had stood perfectly still while Carl filled the cup of insults to the brim, seeking to break Brian's spirit by words. And Brian had done nothing. The pressure had built up in silence.

Before iron melts, it glows red, then white. It is possible to detect, by watching it, just how hot iron is. Dynamite is different.

Brian felt the blow as a heavy impact on his right fist. That was all. His vision cleared, and Carl was back against the doorframe, bent nearly double, his hands over the lower part of his chest. Time stretched out as he leaned there, unable to move.

Into the silence came the voice of the radio announcer, giving the news summary:

". . . disturbing report from Pakistan, where border patrols have picked up a defector who claims to be a Soviet scientist assigned to work at a secret Soviet base in the mountains of Afghanistan. According to the scientist, the work being done in Afghanistan could destroy overnight much of man's accumulated progress for several thousand years."

Brian frowned and glanced at Carl. Carl slowly straightened, murmuring, as if talking to himself, *"One punch."*

The announcer went on, "Unrest in the Middle East flared up again . . ."

Carl was looking at Brian with an expression of dazed wonder, and then of respect.

Brian watched Carl warily, conscious that if he were in Carl's place, he would have to fight. Carl, however, didn't work that way. He grinned and said, "Sorry I jumped on you so hard. But you've got an unfair advantage. You work with Anne all day."

This was so different from what Brian expected that he couldn't seem to get hold of it. Finally he said, "What choice does that leave me? I could either quit working here or get a new assistant. *Naturally,* I work with her. She's a chemist. Why don't you go find yourself a girl electronics technician?"

Carl said apologetically, "I like Anne."

"I don't blame you. But I like Anne."

9

They looked at each other in exasperated bafflement.

In the quiet, they could hear the radio announcer summing up the news headlines.

Carl scowled. "What was that about research in Afghanistan?"

"One of their scientists is supposed to have defected," Brian explained. "He claims they were doing work that could set progress back several thousand years."

"What kind of work?"

"I don't know."

The announcer said, "For further details, listen to our regular newscast at eight . . ."

Carl glanced at Brian. "Were you planning to listen to that?"

"No. Why? Do you think there's something in it?"

"I don't know. There have been rumors of a Russian cryogenics lab in Afghanistan. The rumor is that the Russians and Afghans made a deal. The Russians would put up a dam and hydroelectric project, and the Afghans would let them put up a cryogenics lab and supply it with power from the hydroelectric project."

Brian thought it over. Cryogenics involved the study of extreme cold. At temperatures well below zero, familiar substances acted far differently than usual. Liquid mercury froze solid and could be used to hammer tacks. Hot dogs snapped like sticks. And when the temperature was made low enough—hundreds of degrees below freezing—there were very strange effects. At these extremely low temperatures an electric current had been started in a lead ring, and two years later, it was still flowing. The helium ordinarily used to fill balloons became a liquid that could slip through tiny cracks, and showed strange properties not shared by other substances. In addition, there was a rare variety of helium that didn't show the strange properties. Brian could see why anyone might be interested in such research.

"Why put the lab in Afghanistan?" Brian inquired.

Carl smiled. "To get it out of Russia."

"Explosive?"

"Apparently."

"I wonder what they were doing?"

"That's the question."

"Well, I guess I will listen to the news," Brian mused.

"Would you mind if I listened with you? The chief is in and out of our lab and I don't care to be listening to the radio when he comes through." Nearly all the men called Cardan "chief," to Cardan's occasional exasperation.

"Come on over. But it will probably all boil down to the fact that nobody really knows anything about it."

"Probably." Carl turned to the door. "I'll see you."

"Okay."

Brian scowled. He and Carl were now apparently back on good terms, but none of their problems had been resolved.

Out in the hallway, there was a brisk tap of heels. Brian smiled. The room suddenly seemed brighter, the objects in it clearer. Brian even imagined that the air was scented with the faint fragrance of the handkerchief he'd found earlier.

Chapter 2

Anne Cermak was wearing a white cotton blouse and a black skirt, and the fragrance Brian had only detected on the handkerchief was now subtly pervasive. She was carrying her short navy-blue coat, and with her free hand reached for the light switch as she came in. She looked at Brian in surprise.

The almost painful longing Brian felt when she was away suddenly became pure pleasure; then he noticed that she'd been crying.

She turned away as she closed the door and tried to speak lightly. "You scared me. I'm used to getting here first."

Brian put his hand gently on her shoulder. "What's wrong, Anne?"

11

For a moment she stood intensely still. Then Brian noticed the faint trembling. Carefully, he turned her toward him. She was trying to hold her head straight, but tears were streaming from her tightly shut eyes.

"Anne—" He held her close, and suddenly her face pressed against his shoulder. She cried desperately for a moment, then gently pulled away. "I'm sorry."

"What is it?" he asked, still holding on to her.

Her face twisted. She began to sob, and clung tightly to him. "Oh, Brian, it's Daddy."

Brian had met the elder Cermak, a gaunt, gray-haired man with a surprisingly direct gaze.

"His heart?"

She shook her head and pulled away. She opened her small blue purse, took out a handkerchief, and dried her eyes.

"I don't know what it is. I woke up last night and he was crying. It was the first time in my life I ever heard him do that. And then he thanked me for being a good daughter, and wished we could have had more time together—" She shut her eyes.

Brian frowned, thinking of the several thousand dollars in his bank account. "Anne, can I help? I make fairly good pay, I've had little to spend it on."

"It isn't—" She shook her head. "You'd have to know him. His heart is bad, and maybe that's part of it. They say sometimes there's a strong feeling of anxiety. But this is different. He said he'd had a dream; and he *believed* this dream! It was like a prophecy, and he could see into the future. He told me what would happen, and then he became so deeply depressed he wasn't like the same man. Oh, Brian, what can I *do*?"

For a moment he could think of nothing to say. Then he remembered the talk he'd had with Anne's father one night, on the porch of the old frame house the two had rented on the outskirts of town. Remembering the straightforward conversation, Brian mused, "He seems a sensible, hard-headed man—wait, this happened at *night*?"

"It was dark out. I think it must have been about four."

Brian thought it over. "Sometimes in the middle of the

12

night things seem a lot worse than after the sun is up. He's had an awful lot of hardship, hasn't he?"

She nodded. "But things have been better lately. This is a good job. I make enough for both of us."

Brian remembered Anne saying once that her mother had died when she was very young, and her father had raised her. That must have been no easy job. The elder Cermak had been a coal miner in the mountains of West Virginia, where mechanization and the competition of gas and oil had eliminated many jobs. Without special skills, he could now find little to do. Yet Anne had told Brian that it had not been a scholarship or a loan that had put her through college; her father had done it.

Brian frowned. Maybe the older man was feeling useless now that he was unemployed. Of course, he didn't mope around the house. He had painted the inside, room by room, keeping himself busy during the winter between trips to the employment office. As he jokingly told Brian while showing him the living room he'd just finished painting, "I have to keep myself busy and earn my board." He grinned at his daughter. "I don't want to be a kept man." There had been no resentment in the comment—and yet his inability to earn money had to rankle.

"I can't believe it's anything but a bad night," he assured her. "Possibly he's coming down with some sickness. There's been a lot of flu around. If you want to take the day off and stay with him, I'm sure Mr. Cardan would—"

She shook her head. "It wouldn't help. He all but threw me out of the house, shouting me down when I tried to say I'd stay with him. I got ready for work and went back in to argue with him; he took me by the arms and walked me right to the door. I *couldn't* stay with him."

"Do you want me to drive you out this noon?" Anne usually rode back and forth, in the morning and at night, with a woman neighbor who had a job in a nearby factory.

"No," she said, "he wouldn't like that. But, Brian, could you—if I invited you to dinner tonight—?"

"I'd like to come." He smiled. "You ought to know that."

She said, "If I could only get him to thinking about something else. And he likes you." She looked at Brian with a warm smile and started to say something, but at that moment there was a rap at the door.

Brian remembered that Carl had asked to listen to the news with him. The news was the last thing Brian wanted to listen to at that moment, and Carl was about the last person he wanted to see. But there was nothing to do about it now.

Anne had gathered her things together, and now said to Brian, "Thank you." They smiled at each other for a moment.

The knock at the door was repeated, a little louder and more insistent.

Anne went into the left-hand cubicle to hang her things up, closing the door of the cubicle quietly behind her. Brian glanced at the lab door, and said, "Come in." He looked at his watch. It was a few seconds before eight. Brian could scarcely believe it. He seemed to have lived several weeks since he'd pulled into the parking lot. Actually, a little over half an hour had passed.

Then the lab door opened and a frowning Carl came in. "Anne here?"

"She got in a few minutes ago. Sure you don't want to listen to that news down in your lab? I don't think anyone would hang you for it."

Carl shook his head. "This would be the wrong morning. The chief's in a terrible frame of mind."

"What's wrong?"

"As nearly as I can figure it out, he had a bad dream."

Brian blinked.

Carl said defensively, "I know. It sounds crazy. But he's got Donovan and Maclane tearing around like wild tigers. Come on, let's listen to that news and then I can get back to work."

They went into Brian's cubicle and turned up the volume of the radio. For a moment they were treated to an unctuous voice describing the wisdom of a local firm of stockbrokers. Then there was a news item neither of them were interested in. Brian by this time had lost interest in the news about the Afghanistan cryogenics lab, and walked out to see what he had to do today. He had a check list thumbtacked to a small bulletin board and was glancing at it when he heard the announcer say, "Dr. Wienko said the low-temperature research into the relationship of the structure of Helium Four with its strange properties was only one aspect of the Helmand laboratory's work. Here is a portion of the interview."

". . . Would you say, then, Doctor, that the researches are a danger to the world at large?"

"Not a danger to the world, no. But to civilization as we know it, yes."

"This isn't a question of a great explosion, a great deal of destruction?"

"You don't need a great explosion to create a great deal of destruction. Take modern industry and break the wires that bring electricity to the factories. That is all you need to do. If you can keep the wires broken, the industry is as useless as if you blew it up with a hydrogen explosion. No, this is not a question of an explosion. It is an entirely different kind of thing."

"How is it different?"

"Well, past research has discovered for us laws of nature. Then we have built on these laws of nature."

"And this is different from that?"

"Yes."

"But all science can do, Doctor, is to discover facts, deduce theories, find out which theories are true laws of nature. Isn't that so? How can there be anything different?"

"Because science is not standing still. As we work down closer to the core of things, we discover that our first conclusions were naïve. We did not know as much as we thought we knew. We assumed that when we found a law of nature, it was invariable. That was ignorance on our part."

"Do you mean that a law of nature is—that it can be changed?"

"That is right. We have here the key to pursuade nature to do things differently, in a limited region of space. But this is dangerous. It is like undermining the ground on which you have your house."

"Might this be a key to antigravity, as it's called?"

15

"It might, but that is a comparatively constructive use. What I speak of are certain processes in nature that are more vulnerable to interference than we realized. On some of these processes, we have built our present civilization. And as we have built, we have cast aside what went before. Consider the position of electricity at present. If electricity should fail, what would happen to our civilization?"

"And you believe that these experiments could cause electrical trouble?"

"I have no doubt of it. It has happened before. On one occasion, we had already a temporary failure of electrical power in an approximately circular region with a radius of more than nine kilometers."

"Did you object at that time to the experiments?"

"Not at all. The experiments are very necessary."

"Then why do you object now?"

"We have made improvements and refinements in the apparatus. The vacuum is harder, the temperatures lower, the materials purer. My colleagues feel that this will make a noticeable but not large change. My studies convince me that, on the contrary, there will be a marked and decisive change. The radius of the surface area affected will be on the order of one thousand times as great. Possibly the effect will show new characteristics when it occurs on so large a scale. In any event, the result will be the destruction of civilization as we know it. Modern industrial civilization is in great danger at this moment."

The voice cut off, and the announcer said, "That report came from Pakistan, where a Soviet scientist has just defected to the West. There was fresh trouble in the Middle East last night—"

Brian turned off the radio.

Carl said, "He claims that their experiment is likely to cause widespread power failure? Is that right?"

"As nearly as I could tell, he claims it will cause widespread *irreparable* power failure."

"Then I guess we wasted time listening to it," Carl countered. "There *is* no irreparable power failure."

Carl looked around, obviously wondering where Anne was.

A pounding of heavy heels going past in the hall outside attracted their attention.

"Oh-oh," said Carl. "It sounds like something is going on out there. I'd better get back in circulation."

The minute he'd hurried out, Anne opened the door of her little office. Her face was very pale.

Brian, alarmed, said, "What is it, Anne?"

For a moment she seemed unable to speak, then she said, "Brian, that's what Daddy's dream was about."

It took Brian a few moments to realize what she meant. "Listen," he said, "does your father have a radio in his room?"

"Yes, he has a little portable I got him last Christmas."

"Could he have left it on last night?"

"I suppose so. Why?"

"Suppose he were lying there, slightly feverish, and the radio wasn't turned all the way off. Then, suppose this report came on and he heard it just as he fell asleep. He could very well have imagined he dreamed it."

She said, "That *could* be it. He might have turned the volume control way down without remembering to actually turn the switch." She sounded relieved. "That *could* have happened."

Brian said, "I don't claim to know much about electronics, but according to Carl there is no way to permanently cut off electrical power."

Anne smiled. "That's a relief to me. I'm sorry I made such a fuss."

Brian smiled. "Is my dinner invitation still good?"

"You know it is."

"Well, let's see what we have to do today." He crossed the room to study his check list. Anne came over to stand beside him. Brian felt the sense of deep contentment that rarely comes to a man, and seldom lasts long even then. He had a job that he enjoyed, in a company that he wanted to work for, and Anne, he realized with a wonderful certainty, liked him—just as he liked her. For a moment, everything seemed perfect.

And then, overhead, the lights went out.

Anne's hand gripped his arm. Brian frowned, opened the door, and glanced out in the hall. The hall lights were out.

Anne said, "Oh, Brian. I'm afraid."

"It may be just a local power failure. Let's see if there's anything about it on the radio."

He snapped on the portable radio. Nothing happened. He turned the volume control high and swung the tuning knob from one end of the dial to the other.

There was no sound.

He clicked the radio off, then on again. Still no sound. He picked up the phone that sat on his desk. There was no hum, buzz, or sound of any kind.

He dialed the operator. Nothing. He realized that his heart was hammering, and that he was on the edge of panic.

With an effort, he compelled himself to breathe slowly and steadily, calmly, and to sit down and methodically think things over.

Anne was watching him tensely.

Merely looking at her was such a pleasure to Brian that abruptly his sense of tension snapped, and he could think clearly. He said, "Don't you have a little flashlight you carry in your purse?"

"Yes," she said.

"Would you get it? And I should have a big one here in this desk, somewhere."

Brian was thinking that lights could be cut off by a power failure, and so could a number of broadcasting stations, if the failure were widespread enough, but flashlights carried their own power with them.

He slid open the drawers of his desk, looking for his flashlight.

Anne came back from her cubicle, a stricken look on her face. She was holding a little pocket flashlight. "It doesn't work. The light doesn't work any more."

Brian suddenly realized that the anguish in her voice was not for the bulb that didn't light. She was undoubtedly thinking of her father's dream.

Brian found his flashlight, tipped it so he could see the bulb, and pressed the switch forward. The bulb remained dark.

Brian took the batteries out. He remembered putting them in, fresh, not long before. He hadn't used the light enough for the batteries to grow weak, and so far as he could tell from looking at them, there was nothing wrong. He tried the flashlight using an extra bulb; it still didn't work. He was putting it back in the desk drawer when he realized that, for some reason, the flashlight felt strange.

Puzzled, Brian took it out and looked at it. The finish looked somewhat dull and lusterless, but then, though the batteries and bulb were new, he'd had the flashlight itself for several years. He felt the smooth surface of the metal, couldn't pin down what was wrong, and impatiently put the flashlight back in the drawer.

Anne still stood in the doorway, holding the little pocket flashlight. Her face showed concern.

Before Brian could say anything, the lab door opened.

Carl, his face tense, said, "Brian, Anne, the chief wants you."

Cardan, a powerfully built man who looked to be in his middle forties, was seated at his desk, a smoldering stub of cigar clenched in one corner of his mouth. On the desk were a couple of dry cells, cut open; a flashlight, taken apart; and a glass jar with two metal strips immersed in a clear solution, a wire running from each of the metal strips to connect with a meter lying on the desk.

Donovan, a tall blond-haired man, was leaning across the desk, examining the connections. A slender, sharp-featured man named Maclane, standing beside Donovan, said to Cardan, "You *dreamed* this would happen?"

Cardan put the smoldering stub of his cigar in the ash tray, and, scowling, pulled open a desk drawer and selected a fresh cigar. He lit it from the stub, sat for a moment blowing out a cloud of smoke, then shook his head.

"What I dreamt was this nightmare, all right. Electricity vanished from the face of the earth—" He seemed bewildered. "We've got to find out what's going on." He glanced up, nodded to Brian and Anne, then glanced back at Maclane.

"Mac, suppose you get some men started checking every

form of electricity. Try every electrical power source—
battery, generator, magneto—whatever you can think of.
If that doesn't work, try generating static electricity. Go
at it from every angle conceivable."

"I'll get right to it," Maclane said on his way out.

Cardan glanced at Donovan. "Don, suppose you circulate
around and find out about *other* energy sources. You might
start by checking our experimental cars down in the lot.
That lightweight gas turbine and the new steam engine ought
to be down there. See how they work."

"Okay, Chief."

Carl, Anne and Brian came in as Donovan went out.
Cardan glanced at Anne, his expression softening slightly.
"Can you run a series of standard chemical reactions to see
if, from a chemist's viewpoint, everything is apparently
normal and as it should be?"

Anne nodded

Cardan said, "Good. Go to it."

Anne hurried out of the room. Cardan eyed Brian and
Carl for a moment. "You two feel tough?"

Carl grinned. "Hard as nails, Chief."

Brian noticed the glint in Cardan's eyes. There was
something about the way Cardan sat there, speculatively
watching them, the smoking cigar in his raised hand, that was
a challenge.

"What," said Brian, "did you have in mind?"

Cardan drew on the cigar, and blew out a cloud of smoke.
"The news this morning told of a Russian lab in Afghanistan, and of one of their men who quit, claiming what they
were doing in the lab might knock out electricity a long distance away. Not too long after that, our lights, phone, and
radio went off, and we haven't been able to raise so much as
a dull glow in any piece of electrical apparatus since. It's
natural to put two and two together and conclude the
Russian lab is responsible. But Afghanistan is a long distance from here. Before we jump to conclusions, we want
to know what it's like *outside*. We need to know if the
electricity has been knocked out all over the city. If it is,
what things will be like out there after this goes on for a

while is hard to say. I want a pair of men to go out there and see what's going on. Are you willing?"

"I'm willing," Brian agreed.

Carl said, "Sure."

"Okay," said Cardan. "Look around and see if you can get some idea just how far this lack of electricity extends. There are bound to be effects we wouldn't think of offhand. Find out all you can. See how people are reacting. Then get back and let us know."

Brian and Carl nodded their agreement at the same time, and turned toward the door.

Cardan called, "Wait a minute."

They turned around.

Cardan said, "Stick together out there. Don't get separated. We don't know yet what it may be like."

Carl said, "If we split up, we could cover ground twice as fast."

"Sure," said Cardan, "but my idea was to get you both back afterwards."

"I don't think there'd be any trouble," Carl said. "At least, not yet."

"How are you going to get around?"

Brian said, "That's right. If electricity is knocked out, there goes the ignition system of cars."

"Yeah," Carl agreed. "But I know a place where we can rent bicycles."

Cardan said, "Assuming cars *are* stopped, and the view out the window over there looks like it, there are going to be a lot of people on foot, and some of them aren't going to like it."

"Hm," said Carl. "Yes, I see what you mean. Maybe the two of us *had* better stick together."

"I think so. And keep your eyes open." He smiled. "Good luck."

"Thanks, Chief." They turned, nodded to a wiry man with black hair combed straight back, and went out. Behind them, they could hear Cardan say exasperatedly, "Smitty, do I look like an Indian, or the head of a fire department?"

"I don't know, Chief," said Smitty. "Why do you ask?"

21

Carl and Brian glanced at each other and grinned. But in the dim hall, lit only by the light coming from the open doors of occasional labs, their faces had a shadowy, sinister look. It occurred to Brian that the situation wasn't yet real to either of them. As they walked by the closed door of the lab where he and Anne worked, it occurred to Brian that if electricity *was* gone, so was his job. So much of the work done by Research East involved electronics that, without that work, the company couldn't survive.

And then Brian realized that it was a lot worse than that, that this thought only began to scratch the surface. It was with a vague feeling of dread that he followed Carl into the dark interior of the elevator.

Carl stopped abruptly. "My mistake." The elevator, being electric, obviously could no longer run.

Brian said, "Let's try it anyway."

Carl felt through his pockets, found a book of matches, and struck a light. Brian held his breath, and punched the button to take them to the ground floor.

Nothing happened.

Carl shrugged. "Worth a try."

"Yeah. Well, the stairs are around the corner there."

They walked around the bend in the hall; the box over the door that usually glowed red, spelling "Exit," was dark now. Carl pulled open the door and Brian followed him quickly down the steps. At the ground floor, where the door opened out into the parking lot, Carl hesitated.

"Somehow, I'm not anxious to go out there," he said, his usually pugnacious face bleak.

Brian paused before the closed door. "By the time we get back, things may seem a lot different."

For a moment they both stood silent, then Brian said, "But things are going to change whether we go out there or not."

"I suppose so."

Then, as if by common consent, they pushed open the door.

Chapter 3

Cool spring air chilled their faces as they stepped out onto the parking lot. A gust of wind blew several pages of a newspaper, folding and unfolding, across the blacktop, to press them flat against the link fence. Then they were out of the shadow of the building and the sun was warm as they walked toward the gate.

Donovan's voice came to them from a car backed part way out in the lot. "Mind trying your cars before you leave?"

Brian thought for an instant that perhaps they'd been mistaken, and it *was* only a local power failure. Then he saw the puff of steam blow away in the cool air as the car glided forward. That was the experimental steam car, and all it used electricity for was lights, accessories, and a device that could be used to ignite the pilot which, in turn, lit the main burner. But a match would do the job just as well.

Carl and Brian waved their assent to Donovan and split up to go to their own cars.

Brian slid into his car, put the key in the ignition and turned it. Ordinarily there was a faint *clunk* noise from somewhere in the machinery as he turned on the ignition. But now there was silence.

Brian turned the key further, to switch on the starting motor. The only sound was of the wind blowing past. The car remained silent.

Brian tried again, and then once more. Nothing happened.

He looked at the clock on the dashboard, stopped at nineteen after eight. He tried the dome light without success, then glanced at the ammeter and turned the headlight switch on. The ammeter needle stayed dead on zero. He snapped on the radio and the only sound was the click of the pushbutton. Habit led him to turn off the useless switches before he got out. Then he stood, one hand on the door, the cold wind whipping his trouser legs about his

23

ankles, and abruptly he asked himself: *How* could *all these things stop working?* The car battery was separate from any other source of electric power. The car was self-contained, and as long as the generator kept the battery charged, it, in turn, would supply current to start the motor and run all the car's accessories. How *could* anything affect this self-contained power supply?

Scowling, Brian opened the hood and checked the connections of the battery cables. They were tight and clean. He got out a pair of pliers, spread their handles wide, wrapped his handkerchief around the wide-open jaws, and pressed the end of one handle to the positive terminal of the battery. Cautiously, he swung the pliers to touch the tip of the other handle to the battery's negative terminal.

Nothing happened.

Brian rubbed and pressed the bare metal against the battery terminals. There was no spark, no sign of life from the battery.

He put the pliers away, took a last look under the hood, lowered it, and locked the car door.

Across the lot, Carl slammed down the hood of his car, tossed about eight feet of cable with clamps on both ends into the trunk, and crossed the lot, the sun glinting on his blond hair, his pale blue eyes narrowed in exasperation.

"Any luck?" he called.

"All bad," said Brian.

Carl nodded dispiritedly.

Donovan was just climbing out of another car. He called to them, "How did it go?"

Carl held both hands up with his thumbs down.

Donovan waved his hand in thanks. Brian and Carl headed toward the gate.

"It acts," said Carl, "exactly like a dead battery. The question is, *is* it a dead battery?"

"I couldn't raise a spark," said Brian.

"Me either. But what could make the charge leak away that fast?"

"Ionized air?"

"Maybe. Or a conducting surface layer on the battery. But where would *that* come from?"

"According to the news—what was it?—a law of nature can be changed."

Carl's lips tightened. "Something like that. I think he said, 'We have here the key to lead nature to do things another way, in a limited region of space.' That was the sense of it."

"Yes," said Brian. "There was more, too. Something about, if you could break the wires that carry electricity to factories, and keep the wires broken, the factories would be just as useless as if you blew them up with an H-bomb."

"Break the wires," said Carl. "Did he mean make actual breaks in the wires, or was it just a figure of speech?"

"The trouble is," Brian said, "we don't have enough to go on."

They were through the gate now, on the sidewalk. In front of them, in the street, opposite the entrance to the parking lot, sat a motionless car. About twenty feet behind it was another motionless car, its hood raised. Both vehicles were empty. People were hurrying along the sidewalk, their faces baffled or angry. At a curbside phone booth, a well-dressed man irritably jiggled the hook of the dead phone. "Hello? Hello! *Operator*!" The traffic light over the intersection ahead swayed in the wind, its three lenses dark.

Snatches of conversation flew past like the bits of paper that blew along the sidewalk.

". . . have to get there by ten, but am I going to *do* it?"

". . . place is going to be a disaster area by this time tomorrow if this goes on . . ."

". . . So? It's a vacation. How *could* I get to work? I'll watch TV . . ."

At the corner, two lines of cars, headed in opposite directions, were drawn up as if waiting for the light. On the intersecting street, the cars were spread out, one halfway through the intersection, another making a right turn, just outside the crosswalk, as if waiting for a pedestrian. Most of the cars were empty, but here and there stood one with its hood up, the exasperated owner leaning in to check connections or tighten wires.

Carl led the way around the corner and they walked up a few blocks, through a district of small stores. Here the owners, wearing aprons or suitcoats, stood in the doorways of the darkened shops. Outside a small tavern, a burly bartender was frowning heavily and talking with several customers sipping beer.

"Sure," he was saying, as Brian and Dave passed. "This isn't the first time the lights went out on me. Or the TV. But what about the traffic? How do you explain that?"

A few doors away they sighted a store with new bicycles out on the sidewalk.

Carl said, "Here we are," and they went inside. A thin, gray-haired man joked with Carl for a few minutes, then agreed to rent them two bicycles for seventy-five cents each, till early afternoon. The owner grinned. "Seeing it's you, Carl. For anyone else, I'd charge a buck and a half, at least. I've got the only wheels in town that work."

"Better not charge me a buck and a half," said Carl. "Or the next time your TV quits—" He drew a finger across his throat.

The proprietor laughed. "Okay, Bring them back in good shape. Speaking of TV, have *you* got any idea what's wrong?"

"Beyond me. Maybe a sudden ionization of the air let the charge flash out of car batteries and grounded a lot of wires." He glanced at the battered bicycles. "What do you mean, bring them back in good shape? You want us to do a repair job?"

The proprietor responded with a cheerful insult and then they were out in the street.

The scene, as they pedaled toward the river and the bridge leading out of town, remained about the same; but, seen on a larger scale, because they were going faster, it became alarming. Endlessly, they raced past cars to their left, while to their right the people mingled on the sidewalks, some hurriedly trying to keep appointments, others milling aimlessly. As they passed through the main shopping district, pedestrians overflowed the sidewalks, and Brian and Carl swerved to flash down the white line in the center, passing stalled cars and trucks on either side of them. Then they were pedaling up the gently arching bridge over the river.

Brian had let Carl lead the way, but now he pedaled harder and pulled up beside him.

"North Hill?"

Carl thought a moment, then nodded. "Good view from there."

They shot down a little-traveled side street and raced down comparatively deserted roads where only a few cars were stalled, and only a few puzzled people walked, frowning, beside low buildings and wooden fences. Then they were on a road that led into town from the hills outside.

Carl, leaning forward, his blond hair blown back by the wind, big hands gripping the handle bars, grinned at Brian suddenly.

"Race?" he challenged.

Something about the fresh country air, the brisk wind, the bright sun, and invigorating exercise after the tensions of the morning, gave Brian a sense of boyish pleasure.

"Why not?"

"To the overpass."

"Okay."

Carl spurted forward. Brian, grinning, raced after him. Using a trick that had served him well in the past, Brian began to breathe hard, well before he needed to.

Carl glanced back over his shoulder. "What's the matter, Grandpop? Out of shape?"

Brian, the exhilarating extra oxygen pouring through his system, began to pedal harder. Carl glanced ahead, then glanced back, surprised. Brian was edging up on him. Already the front wheel of Brian's bicycle was level with the rear wheel of Carl's.

Carl fixed his gaze on the bridge coming into view a half mile up the road, and pedaled mercilessly.

Brian, his attention fastened on the front wheel of Carl's bike, willed the distance to shorten, then focused his thoughts on the rhythm of his legs and lungs. For a moment he was conscious of nothing but the wind hard on his face, then vaguely conscious that he was drawing forward, moving slowly and steadily ahead of the man and the bicycle beside him. Carl became aware of this, too, and for a moment he began to pull away.

It seemed to Brian that there was nothing more he could do, but from somewhere inside him came an unexpected determination that brought him forward again, and then side by side, the two of them flashed over the overpass and up the first rise of the road that branched off to lead up the side of North Hill.

After a hard uphill climb, Brian and Carl, breathing heavily, leaned the bicycles against two trees at the edge of a graveled parking place where in the summer cars often stopped to look south over the city. Among the trees were green-painted picnic benches and stone fireplaces, and Brian and Carl, each casting secret yearning glances at the benches, yet neither willing to admit to the other how worn, weak, and tired he felt, walked unsteadily through the picnic grounds, past occasional patches of grainy snow that lay in hollows and behind fallen logs, where the sun couldn't reach till it rose so high that the branches of the thick hemlocks no longer intervened. Underfoot, the ground felt soft and springy, and Brian was afraid that if he stepped a little too abruptly, both knees might give way and he would land flat in the snow.

"Ah," said Carl, his mouth opened only slightly in order to disguise the sound of heavy breathing, "here we are."

Brian made his own voice as steady as he could. "Yes. Here we are."

Spread out below them was a wide, clear view of the city, the highway curving into view from the side, sweeping across in front of them, then swinging away in a wide, gentle circle to disappear on the other side. The scene was clear, and so plainly different from what either of them had ever seen from this vantage point, they both forgot the need to appear invincible, and sank down on a large, gently sloping granite rock on the edge of the hill.

From here they could see the city, the river curving through it, shining here and there in the bright sun, and the railroad tracks between road and river.

This much, they'd both seen before.

But the motionless cars and trucks dotted endlessly along the highways, the people trudging along the side of the road, the long freight train dead still on the tracks, the thick pall of smoke pouring from the factory chimneys, the tail of of a crashed plane just visible in the wreckage of a burning house near the edge of town—all this was different.

After a few minutes Brian and Carl had both recovered their breath, and they were both still staring at the scene. All through town, and as far as the eye could see, no single car or truck, large or small, was moving.

Brian said, "There's nothing local about this."

"No. And seeing it all at once, it looks worse."

Brian glanced at the smoke pouring from the factory chimneys.

"Why so much smoke?"

"They use electric precipitators to collect the smoke particles. With the electricity out, the precipitators don't work."

Brian looked from the chimneys to the highway. Unlike the situation in a traffic jam, the cars were well spread out. Some few were pulled to the side, but most were still in the traffic lanes.

Carl got to his feet a trifle unsteadily.

"Well, we've seen what we came for."

"Wait a minute," said Brian. "Let's be sure we understand what we see."

"The main thing is, nothing's moving. No motors work. That's what the chief wanted to know."

"Maybe," said Brian, trying to keep the sarcasm out of his voice, "*you* can see and digest the whole thing without thinking it over, but *I* can't."

"What is it," said Carl, sarcasm creeping into his voice, "that you'd like explained to you?"

"To begin with," said Brian, "that train—" He paused, startled, as he saw something out of the corner of his eye.

Down on the highway, at the extreme right, something large was moving. "Forget the train. Take that for a starter. Explain *that* to me."

Carl, on his feet a few paces back from Brian, stepped forward and bent to see under the low limb of a nearby hemlock.

"I don't see—" He paused, blank-faced.

Down on the highway, a huge truck was steadily weaving

its way in and out amongst the stalled cars. It slowed, edged up to two cars abreast, shoved the left-hand one well forward out of the way, then backed and came ahead again to weave through between them. A puff of black smoke drifted up from its vertical exhaust. The sun shone in a brief flash on the lettering giving the trucking company's name.

The truck slowed, stopped, and one of the drivers jumped out to take the wheel of a car slewed across the road. The grind of gears was plainly audible as the truck eased forward, pushed the car to the edge of the road, backed and filled, picked up the driver who'd gotten out, then eased ahead again.

Carl nodded slowly. "It's a diesel. That explains it."

Brian said, "The compression of the fuel and air fires it, and they don't use spark plugs?"

"Right. I think some of them use a spark at the beginning, when the engine's cold, but after it heats up they don't need that. And, of course, the engine's hot now."

The truck was creeping past. People at the side of the road were shouting to the driver, apparently asking for rides to the nearest town, but the driver shook his head and kept going down the highway.

"How," said Brian, puzzled, "do they start those things?"

Carl thought for a moment. "I *think* they start the same as any other car, with an electric starting motor."

"In that case, as long as the engine runs, they're all right. But if they turn it off, it's dead, and that's the end of it?"

Carl ran a hand through his yellow hair. It was plain from his look of chagrin that Carl was remembering his own confident statement that they'd seen everything they needed to know.

Brian, wrestling with the problem the truck presented, was only vaguely aware of Carl's discomfort. As far as Brian was concerned, the only thing that mattered was to get the clear picture of the situaion as Cardan had requested. And as far as Brian was concerned, he knew that *his* picture wasn't clear yet.

"How about that train?" he said. "That's a diesel, isn't it?"

"Yes, it is."

"Wouldn't it fire by compression, the same as the truck?"

"Yes, but they're actually electric trains. The diesel engines turn generators, and the electricity that's generated runs the electric motors which turn the wheels."

Brian looked at the trucks stalled here and there along the road. He could see at least one of them, close behind a small foreign-made car, that hid the upright stack of a diesel.

Carl, his expression alert, had noticed the same thing. "Looks like that one almost ran into the car in front."

Brian nodded. "He probably stopped in a hurry, took one look around—"

"And he'd naturally be dumfounded to see all the cars stopped at once," Carl continued. "No doubt, people would start getting out. If he'd had his radio on, all of a sudden all the stations would go off."

"He might think it was an atomic attack."

"He'd yank on the brake, turn off the ignition, and take a flying dive for the nearest ditch."

"Then, when nothing happened and he came back, the engine wouldn't start."

Carl looked at Brian with a puzzled expression, then frowned and looked down again at the highway. The diesel that was still running was out of sight now. The people were still walking along the edge of the highway, a few scrambling up the bank to the overpass Brian and Carl had crossed, and heading into town.

"*Now* haven't we seen everything?" Carl asked.

Brian looked around and spotted a medium-sized white oak about fifty feet away. "If we climb that tree over there, couldn't we see over these evergreens?"

"Sure, but—you mean, so we could see further down the road?"

"Yes."

"What's the point of that? We'll just see more of the same."

"How do we know?"

Carl started to speak, then changed his mind. Scowling, he led the way to the oak. He turned to say something, then

31

shrugged, took hold of a low limb, and pulled himself up into the tree.

Brian waited till Carl was up in the tree and out of the way, then took hold of a small limb, feeling the rough bark under his fingers, pulled himself up, got his feet onto a limb nearby, stood up to grip another limb overhead. The dead, brown, violet-tinged leaves still clinging to the limbs rustled around him as he climbed.

At last they were above the level of the young hemlocks and could look out onto a stretch of highway that reached far out into the distance. As far as the eye could see, the sun shone on the smooth hoods, roofs, and front windows of stalled cars spread out along the highway.

"See," said Carl. "What did I tell you?"

"Yes," said Brian. "You were right. But now we *know* it."

Carl flushed slightly, started angrily to speak, then stopped. Ruefully, he said, "You've got a point there. I *do* go off half-cocked sometimes."

"I didn't mean—"

"Maybe not, but it's so. That's something in your favor."

Brian failed to get the point, but Carl reminded him, "Remember, we both want the same girl."

"Sure, but can't we leave that up to her?"

"Suppose you thought *I* was going to get her?"

"I wouldn't be happy. But—she could do worse."

Carl looked blank for an instant, then grinned. "Thanks. But how does that help *you*? You like her, don't you?"

"Of course I like her."

"Then how," said Carl, looking puzzled, "could you give her up?"

Brian exasperatedly started to speak. He was going to say: *I don't own her. Neither of us do. How do I give up something I don't have.* But he saw this wasn't what Carl meant. Slowly, Brian said, "I've lost things before."

For a brief instant Carl looked sympathetic. Then he shook his head. "That's the difference between you and me. I always get what I want."

"Even—" Brian began.

"By hook or by crook," said Carl positively, his light-blue eyes frank and clear. "I *win*. I've *got* to."

Brian looked off in the distance for a moment. He, too, had an outlook on life, picked up in the bruising punishment that had come about before he learned it, and he could put it in a few words, just as Carl could put *his* philosophy in a few words. But something warned Brian that this wasn't the time. Instead, he smiled suddenly and looked at Carl.

"What happens if two guys like you meet head-on? Something gets broken?"

Carl grinned. "We try to avoid each other."

Brian laughed. They took a final look around, then climbed down the tree, dropped to the ground, wincing as the impact put strain on their sore legs, and headed back for the bicycles.

Brian, smiling, said, "Race back?"

"Ouch," said Carl. "Let's just see how far we can coast."

"I wonder if we could put the bikes out of sight by the side of the road on that last curve, then walk down and ask some of those people about the cars. You know, what it was like when they stalled?"

Carl thought a long moment. "Worth a try."

They left the bikes in the trees by the road and asked the people coming up from the highway about what had happened. The answer was always the same:

"The engine just *stopped*, that's all. And then *nothing* worked. Starter, lights, horn, radio—the whole business was dead. So we got out and walked."

Brian and Carl got their bicycles and went back into twon. On the way through town they could see the trouble building up.

In the streets, with their motionless cars and dead traffic signals, without the usual faint sounds of radios playing, and of juke boxes in the background, with the television sets dark, the lights and electricity gone, and the phones dead, with the novelty of the thing starting to wear off, and the fact that it was going to have to be lived with beginning to dawn, with the familiar tools and comforts missing, and uncertainties and vague horrors beginning to loom, people were instinctively gathering together.

The little groups Brian and Carl had seen earlier were big groups now. They stood about on the sidewalks, some staring glumly and others talking excitedly while they looked around at the dead neon signs, really noticing for the first time the gray untended structures that rose up behind the shiny storefronts. They looked down the streets where no cars or buses ran, for the first time seeing a mile as a mile, not as a vague distance to be overcome via a token handed to the driver, a few steps to an empty seat, and a five-minute wait. Other little mobs of people had taken over neighborhood grills or soda fountains, invited in by special prices as worried proprietors cut down the stocks of food and ice-cream that wouldn't keep with electric refrigerators and freezers off. And once the crowds gathered, they stayed there, no one anxious to leave his own, now-familiar group to walk down the nearly empty sidewalk. In a crowd, there was warmth, campanionship. Outside, the silent city, with its main life-current cut off, seemed strange and alien, and the atmosphere had the stillness that came before a thunderstorm.

Past these uneasy, tentatively waiting groups of people, Brian and Carl pedaled with casual slowness, their expressions unconcerned. No one made any hostile gesture toward them. A few people called, "Hey, taxi!" or "Pretty good, no battery." Brian and Carl grinned back and said nothing, but the perspiration on their brows wasn't just from the exertion of pedaling the bikes.

The tension of potential trouble was growing in the air, though the people in those groups waiting in occasional stores might not know it. They saw only each other, whereas Brian and Carl saw the city. So far, nothing really irreversible had happened. Let the power come on again in a few hours, and it would just be an event that stood out, like Hurricane Hazel, or The Blizzard. It would be referred to in later days as The Power Failure, an event more unusual than natural disasters, but on the whole less harmful. It would be made into a joke by entertainers on TV. Magazine articles would be written to describe the way it came about, and how it ended.

But what if the power failure *didn't* end in a few hours?

From somewhere came the smell of smoke, and up ahead Brian saw perspiring men in firemen's uniforms carry past a long ladder, axes, and a length of hose. In a moment, they vanished up a side street.

When the fire trucks won't run, what can the fireman do? Who has more power then, the fire company, or the man with a match?

Brian and Carl glanced at each other, their faces deadly serious. Then they forced smiles, and kept pedaling slowly, casually, back toward the Research East building.

Around them in the city, the pent-up hysteria slowly mounted.

Chapter 4

Brian and Carl left the bicycles where they'd rented them and started back on foot to the Research East building. The crowds in the doorways watched them in blank or speculative silence, and once they were stopped by men anxious for news—any news—who listened avidly as Brian and Carl told of cars stalled far up the highway.

At the Research East entrance, the gate was shut, with an ominous black cable looped and coiled inside, and a sign, "Danger—High Voltage," warning off people who might drift in and cause trouble later on.

Smitty, his black hair combed straight back as usual, opened the gate for them and grinned. "Maybe we can't do anything else with electricity, but it'll still scare people. Go right up, the chief's waiting for you."

Wearily they climbed the four flights of steps to the top floor, and the last flight of steps seemed as long as the other three put together.

"All it used to take," said Carl wonderingly, "was to push a button."

"That was just this morning."

"It seems like years ago—in another world."

Brian said, "Maybe Maclane and Donovan have figured something out."

"Maybe. But taking electricity away from civilization is like taking the framework out of a building. You have to find a substitute awful fast or the whole thing will collapse on top of you, and that's the end of that."

They shoved open the doors at the head of the stairs, walked into the corridor, and a few moments later were staggered to see the piles of rifles, shotguns, ammunition in boxes and bandoliers, hunting knives, knapsacks, pack baskets, skis, snowshoes, heavy blankets, axes, canteens, ponchos, coils of rope, gasoline lanterns, kerosene lanterns, cans of meat, heavy paper sacks of flour and sugar, a stack of cigar boxes and cigarette cartons, gasoline and kerosene cans in a long row against the wall, a box two feet deep and about three feet long containing nothing but gloves and mittens in assorted sizes, another containing heavy socks.

Brian and Carl looked at the supplies and whistled.

"Looks like the chief plans on clearing out."

The sound of many voices came, slightly muffled, from the offiice ahead.

They knocked and Cardan's voice called, "Come in."

They pushed open the door of the office. Cardan sat at his desk, a smoldering cigar jutting from one corner of his mouth, a .45 Colt automatic flat on the desk beside him. Maclane was standing in front of the desk, and Donovan was at a table to one side, using a hydrometer to test several six-volt and twelve-volt batteries sitting on the table. Donovan looked up as Carl and Brian came in, Maclane kept talking, and Cardan nodded abstractedly.

Maclane was saying, "Batteries, magnetos and generators just don't work, that's all. The only kind of electricity left, so far as I can see, is static electricity. You can still take a glass rod, rub it with a cloth, touch two pith balls hung close by on threads, and they'll spring apart. But try to pass a current through a wire and you get nowhere."

"Take a look at this," suggested Donovan. He was using the hydrometer on one of the cells of a six-volt battery. The fluid from this battery tested out as "fully charged."

36

"Almost thirteen hundred," said Donovan. "But now look."

He took a flat metal bar, laid it across the clean shiny terminals of the battery—and nothing happened.

"It's not a question of the charge leaking away, after all. If it were, that battery would be dead," mused Brian.

Carl agreed, staring at the battery, then looking at the hydrometer. "Mind if I try that?"

"Go ahead."

Carl repeated Donovan's procedure and got the same result.

Maclane was saying, ". . . no *conduction*. The trouble seems to be that, for some reason, the electrons are more firmly bound to the metal atoms, so the 'electron gas' that ordinarily carries an electric current in a wire just doesn't exist any more. Or, perhaps, it exists but it's nowhere near as free-moving as it used to be. It's as if that damned Helmand lab sent out a signal that threw a switch inside the atoms—made a minute rearrangement of some kind."

There was a knock at the door. Cardan called "Come in," and Anne Cermak, wearing a light-gray lab coat, stepped into the room. Brian crossed to her immediately and she welcomed him with a smile.

Carl looked up from the battery, saw Brian and Anne talking, and he studied Brian intently for a moment, his eyes lit with a pale glow. Abruptly, he blanked his face and looked back at the battery.

Brian was conscious only of Anne, whose smile faded as she asked, "Is it bad out there?"

"Not yet," said Brian. "But it's getting bad." He realized why she was worried, and said, "Anne, I'll try to get out to see your father after we're through here."

She started to speak but was interrupted by Cardan. "How did things turn out? Notice any changes in chemical tests or reactions?"

"No," said Anne, "everything seemed the same. Except— sometimes the color of a reagent seemed slightly different. But it could have been the lack of electric light in the lab."

"But the reactions themselves seemed the same?"

"Yes, sir."

37

"If you hadn't been particularly watching for differences, would you have noticed any?"

Anne thought a moment. "No, I don't think I would have."

Cardan turned to Brian. "What's it like out there?"

"Getting bad," said Brian. He described much of what they'd seen. He told of the silent, waiting groups, the ominous quiet of the city, and the growing tension. "It looks like a powder keg waiting for a match."

"That's the same impression we've had," Cardan said, "even though we've stayed fairly close. Any sign of electricity?"

"None that we could see." Brian described the firemen headed for the fire, on foot. "And as far as we could see from North Hill, no cars were moving."

Carl cut in. "There was a diesel truck moving."

Cardan looked at the smoking tip of his cigar, and there was a moment's silence which contained a distinct suggestion of a rebuff. Carl drew his breath in as if to speak, then hesitated.

"Where was this?" Cardan wanted to know.

"On the highway." Carl described it in careful and accurate detail.

Brian, listening closely, remembered that he, Brian, had seen this truck after Carl had insisted that they might as well go back, and that there was nothing more to be seen. Brian now listened to Carl describe it very much as if he, Carl, had been the only one to see the truck.

Cardan and the others were listening intently. Maclane looked interested, and Donovan seemed a little excited. Cardan's face remained expressionless.

"So," Carl concluded, "it seems clear that diesel engines are all right while they're running, but I imagine if once they stop, then the electric starting motor won't work."

Maclane straightened up and glanced at Donovan with a faint grin.

Donovan said, "That could be the answer. Rig the engine to start on compressed air."

38

Cardan's face was still expressionless. Carl cleared his throat, but didn't speak. Cardan looked at Carl, a thin wisp of smoke drifting from the cigar he held in one hand.

"Did you see anything else that moved?" There was a faint emphasis on the word "you."

Carl stammered a little as he said, "N-no. We did see a diesel locomotive, but it was stopped."

"What," said Cardan, "did you decide was the reason for that?" Again there was the faintest emphasis on the word "you."

Carl said, "I—we thought it was because the generators and electric driving motors wouldn't work."

Brian suppressed a grin. Carl had taken credit that belonged to Brian, and now, to avoid looking egotistical, Carl was forced to give up credit that really was his own. Brian had forgotten the quickness with which Cardan detected any false note in a man's report.

Cardan had turned to Maclane and Donovan. "Can we fix diesel trucks to start on air?"

"Be a problem," said Donovan. "For one thing, because of the lack of electric power tools. But we've got that portable steam turbine Hooper dreamed up, along with fourteen different sizes of the same thing. Some of them run on LP gas. You remember, Chief, we were trying to sell them as self-powered tools for use away from power lines, up on roofs and so on? And when we had a manufacturer lined up, the mechanic demonstrating the thing got it set up wrong, almost burning his arm off, and before we could get that mess straightened out, self-contained battery-operated tools were on the market."

"The main trouble," said Cardan, "was that the things were bulky."

"That doesn't matter now. And then there's that shuttle-hammer gimmick he worked out, with the little self-contained, reciprocating steam-engine and all the attachments."

Maclane grinned. "That one will really keep your hands warm in cold weather. If it doesn't shake your arms off first."

"Who cares?" said Donovan. "They work."

Cardan blew out a cloud of smoke, smiled, and said, "Steam engines and diesels started by compressed air. Will that do it?"

"Ought to," said Donovan.

"And," said Cardan, "oil and gasoline mantle-lanterns for light?"

Maclane said, "They give a light that can compete for brightness with electricity. But those mantles are fragile. We'd better be sure we've got plenty of spares."

Cardan nodded in agreement, studied the glowing tip of his cigar for a moment, blew out a cloud of smoke, and said, "Good. Now the question is, what do we do? Do we stick around here or do we clear out now?"

"Wait maybe three days," Donovan said, "and this town is going to blow wide-open. Transportation, power and light are gone. To a large extent, heat is knocked out. All of a sudden we've got less capability for actual work and haulage than they had in seventeen-sixty, because then, at least, they had horses and oxen. With this new setup, all of a sudden we just aren't in any shape to care for anywhere near the number of people that are going to have to be cared for. It's going to be every man for himself. And there are a lot of of people in this part of the country."

"Don's right," Maclane agreed. "If we could do any good by staying here, we should stay. But this thing is too big. This isn't a question of a man putting his finger in a hole in the dike and keeping out the flood. It's a question of the whole dike collapsing at once. Anything we might do wouldn't have time to have any effect. We'd just be drowned."

Donovan said, "Let's head for Montana, Chief. That's less-settled country; they're used to rough conditions there, and we've got our test site there—plenty of buildings and equipment."

Cardan glanced questioningly at Brian and Carl. Brian said, "It's a long trip, but that diesel truck we saw *did* get through. The only thing is, what if, at some section of the road, there was a traffic jam at the time the cars' ignition systems were knocked out?"

"So that," said Cardan, "there is, for instance, one solid mass of cars half a mile long?"

"Yes," said Brian. "Then what do we do?"

Donovan said, "We'll either have to drag them out of the way, or shove them off the road. If we can't get by on the mall or shoulder. We'll want to travel on superhighways, away from the cities, as far as possible."

Maclane said, "It's better than staying here and winding up in a siege."

There was a knock at the door and one of the men from a lab downstairs, his face cut and bleeding, was in the doorway with half a dozen others setting down cartons outside.

"I thought you'd want to know, Chief. They're getting into an ugly mood out there. The idea got around that the electric company is behind all this. It seems they put in an atomic reactor, and it shorted out all the electricity somehow. Everybody went to his car, because the reactor was going to be fixed, and then the cars would start. When it didn't happen, the frustration was too much for some of those guys. They're out there smashing windows and threatening to beat in the brains of anybody in reach. Meanwhile, there's a kind of migration going on—people trying to get home on foot in different directions. Naturally, after they get shoved around a few times by these sore-heads, they're in no mood to be even so much as sneezed at the next time. You can still get through out there, but you've got to keep your eyes open."

"There's another thing to think of," Cardan said. "Did you ever read that story about the lady and the tiger?"

"What do you mean, Chief?"

"A man is taken prisoner and put in an arena that has two doors. If he opens one door, a beautiful woman will be waiting inside. If he opens the other, a hungry tiger will rip him to shreds. He doesn't know which door has the tiger behind it, but he's got to open one of the doors."

"How does that apply to us?"

"For all we know," said Cardan, "the electricity *may* come back on again."

"In which case," said Maclane, "if we've done anything really effective to take care of ourselves—"

41

Donovan finished it for him. "We'll appear to be selfish criminals."

Cardan said, "How are we going to get these diesel trucks? If the phones worked, we could try making arrangements that way. But they *don't* work. To find someone who can sell them to us is going to take time."

"Sure," said Maclane, "and if we pussyfoot around trying to do everything strictly according to the rules, we'll never get done. And if the current doesn't come back on, we'll get swallowed up in the chaos that follows. That isn't going to help anybody."

"And aren't we pretty damn certain the current *isn't* coming back on?" Cardan inquired.

"It certainly looks that way to me," Carl said.

"Okay," Cardan said, "here's what we do. On the other end of this block there's a parking lot that belongs to a large trucking company. They use quite a few diesels. If we knock out the fences between here and there, we can bring those diesels in here without going into the street. First, we must get something that will supply the power to start the engines. Second, we have got to do everything possible to make this legal, and to give the trucking company a fair deal. Third, we've got to be sure we keep a good grip on this building till we've got the trucks equipped, loaded and ready to leave. Fourth, *then* we can start out, taking a route that will let us pick up the families of our own people. That means they're going to have to be notified in advance, and told where to be when we pick them up. Don, ask Miss Bowen if there isn't a map of the city in the files."

Donovan was back in a few minutes, the two men spread the map on the desk, and Cardan said, "Railroad Avenue is wide, and there's not too much traffic on it. Fourteenth Street runs out here through the southwest part of town. Suppose we have our people from that part of town at the intersection of Fourteenth and Railroad Ave?" The two men discussed details.

"Are you prepared to risk your necks again this afternoon?" Cardan asked.

"Yes," said Brian.

"Sure," said Carl.

"We'll have Miss Bowen make a list of the addresses of the families that live in the southwest part of town. While she's doing that, we'll canvass the men to make sure they go along with the idea. You go out and tell the people to be at the intersection of Fourteenth and Railroad Avenue at three in the morning."

"Three in the morning," Brian repeated.

"Right," said Cardan, getting up. "By that time we should be ready, and I hope the mobs will have worn themselves out and be sleeping it off. Now Miss Bowen will get you that list."

Half an hour later, Brian and Carl found themselves on bicycles, riding through a part of town that had been filled with people earlier, but was deserted now. The windows of the cars in the streets were smashed, and a man was lying against the base of a fence, either dead or unconscious. Carl and Brian were both quiet, thinking of the bicycle shop, where they'd found the windows smashed, the bicycles gone, and the owner on a cot in a back room, blood seeping from under a bandage on his head, a .32 revolver in his hand as he lay facing the door.

"Ah," he'd murmured, smiling faintly as Carl came in. "For you, I have a bicycle." He felt in his pockets and pulled out a key. "Here, open up that closet. They cleaned me out, but already I had put away those bikes." He'd explained to the dumfounded Carl how the mob had burst in, shoving and fighting, and flattened him when he'd tried to stop them. But, having thought there might be a heavy demand for bicycles, new or used, when people realized there was no other reasonably quick way to get around, he had already put the battered bicycles Carl and Brian had rented out of sight.

"Big civilized men we are," he'd said sarcastically. "The first time the juice goes off, we have a riot. You give us a week like this and we'll be eating rats and mice and smashing each other's heads in for a can of soup."

"Listen," said Carl, "are you hurt bad?"

"I'll be all right. It's just a smack on the head. But it makes me mad. This civilization we got is like a set of

43

stilts. We think we're high up, big men, but it's only the
stilts, not us. As soon as one of them catches in a hole,
over we go, and when we get up, we're just little men. It's
only the stilts that were big . . ."

They had left the old man, still grumbling his disappoint-
ment in people, and pedaled briskly toward Anne's father's
place, but when they got there he was nowhere to be seen.
They called, but the house was empty. Brian finally turned
to go, then suggested leaving a note.

"Wait," said Carl, as they stood in the kitchen, where the
only sound was the tick of a kitchen clock. "Listen, I
thought I heard somebody moving downstairs."

Brian opened the cellar door, looked down into the darkness, and felt a chill premonition.

He called. "Mr. Cermak?"

Behind him, there was the soft scuff of Carl's foot on
the kitchen floor.

The back of Brian's head seemed to explode in a burst of
lights.

Chapter 5

Brian came to to find Anne's father bathing his face
with a cold wet towel. As the older man's tough, workworn
face showed concern, Brian sat up dizzily and felt the large
tender bump at the back of his head. He had a violent
headache, but it seemed to be something he could get over.
Then he thought of the time and glanced at his watch. The
crystal and face of the watch were smashed.

Steve Cermak noticed Brian's gesture and turned to the
kitchen clock on the shelf near the stove. "Twenty-five
after two," he said. "What happened?"

Brian told him. Cermak shook is head sorrowfully. "I
was out for groceries. I thought of going into town after

Anne, but on foot it's a long walk, and I was afraid I'd go in one way while she came out another way. Then she'd be worried and go looking for *me*. I went upstairs and stretched out for a nap; I woke up a few moments ago, certain I had heard a moan. That's when I came down and found you."

"Yeah, thanks to good old Carl." Brian was reminded that because of his colleague's double-cross, he was now pressed for time. "Listen, I'll have to go ahead on the bicycle and get them to send a truck for you." Brian got to his feet, wincing at the furious headache, and went out to get the bicycle he'd left leaned against the porch steps. Anne's father followed, picking up an oil lantern from the kitchen table.

The bicycle wasn't by the porch steps.

They descended the steps, the lantern casting long swinging shadows on the frost that whitened the lawn and crunched stiffly underfoot. They looked briefly under the porch and behind a nearby hedge, then Cermak said, "While we look, time passes."

"Yes," said Brian, "we'll have to make it on foot."

Cermak went inside and came out carrying two jackets. He tossed one to Brian. "We're about the same size."

"Thanks."

Cermak blew out the lantern and shut the door. They slid down a low bank in front of the house and walked along the road.

Brian said, "We've got a long walk ahead of us—and not too much time to do it in. I'm afraid we'll have to run—"

"Young man, don't you worry about me. If you think we need to run, let's run."

They alternated running and walking down the road, their frosty breath drifting slowly up in the cold air that chilled their faces and made Brian's throat feel raw. Every step he took made his head throb, and the muscles of his thighs, because of the race with Carl, rebelled against further activity. It occurred to Brian that the idea of the race might not have been a spontaneous one. Perhaps Carl had already been planning to leave Brian behind, to be swallowed up in the collapse of civilization, while he, Carl, got away to make a fresh start with Anne. Brian remembered Carl saying, "I always get what I want. By hook or by crook, I *win*."

They rounded a bend in the road. The smell of smoke was suddenly strong in Brian's nostrils. There was the pressure of a hand at his arm.

"Wait," said Anne's father. "What's this?"

Ahead of them was a downhill slope, at the bottom of which were two burning houses, facing each other across the road. A little knot of people was struggling in the road, and to the right, a lone woman was sobbing by a pile of furniture near the curb, where an old car was parked.

It seemed clear to Brian that here was the miserable end of somebody's hopes, but all he felt was exasperation at the thought that their way might be blocked.

"Maybe we can run past them when we get close."

"Okay."

They walked downhill, and when they came near the little knot of struggling people, Brian and Cermak started to race past, well to one side.

As they came abreast, a girl's voice cried, "Help! Oh, *help*!"

Brian had a brief glimpse of a girl's face in the glare of the fire, her eyes wide with terror. Then she was slammed back against the car, and the only sound was the roar and crackle of the flames. One of the men rocked the girl's head to one side with an open-handed slap. The other grabbed the cloth of her jacket.

Cermak and Brian whirled at the same time. Cermak shot his right arm around the neck of the nearer of the two men, yanked him back, getting his left arm around the man's waist. There was a brief pinwheeling motion against the glare of the fire, and the second man's hand shot forward, a glint of steel sparkling momentarily.

Brian slammed the knife-hand aside, pivoted on his heel, and smashed his antagonist on the point of the chin. There was a grunt as the man's head snapped back and he slammed against the fender of the car, off balance, near Cermak. Cermak promptly sank a terrific left-handed blow in the knife-man's midsection, and the fight was all over.

The dark-haired girl, still wide-eyed, trembled with relief. Brian said, "Do you live here?"

"No. I was just passing through."

"Which way are you going?"

She pointed down the road toward the city.

"Then you'd better stick with us, if you can." Brian picked up the knife and handed it to her. "Keep this. You may need it. You close it like this, and press this stud to open it."

"I don't know how to thank—"

"Don't. Let's get out of here. We're in a hurry." Brian spoke more sharply than he'd intended. He wanted to help the girl, but the momentary delay could already have made them late at the rendezvous. A few minutes' polite talk could cost them a two-thousand-mile hike.

A few moments later Brian and the older man were going down the road, alternately running and walking, the girl coming along behind them, when abruptly Cermak stopped.

"Oh-oh," he murmured. "Wait."

Brian stopped. Ahead of them, from a peculiarly dark place where a row of tall hemlocks cast their shadows across the moonlit road, came a grunting, struggling noise, and Brian could make out the dim outlines of a group of men, some moving around among the trees, others standing around watching two of them fight.

Cermak murmured, "Better go around this," and they made their way off to the side, guiding the girl by the arm, around to the rear of the houses. Then they were back on the road again, but now a cloud covered the moon, making their progress slower. Here the girl thanked them profusely and disappeared up an intersecting road.

Brian and Cermak were now in a more settled part of town. Encounters with people became more frequent; the roads were more often blocked with cars, and once Brian took a bad fall from a child's roller skate lying on the sidewalk in the dark. When they finally reached the corner of Fourteenth Street and Railroad Avenue, the trucks were gone.

By then, the sky over the city was lit with a red glow. Off to the east, it was just starting to get light.

Anne's father, studying a layer of thin mud at the corner where a large puddle had partly dried up, said, "They've been here, Brian. Even in this light, you can see the marks of big truck tires."

Brian looked around, thinking that Cardan might have left some sign for anyone who reached the spot late. Then he saw the paper tacked to the telephone pole. In the poor light, it took Brian a moment to read it:

Supplies
at R. E.

Anne's father said, "Could we catch up to them at another place in town?"

"I'm afraid not. We'll have to get some supplies, and hope they're held up on the road."

They started out through the city, detouring large groups of people and narrow places, but having to scare off occasional individuals and small groups which made menacing gestures, took a closer look, and generally moved on quickly. By now, their clothes had been torn and dirtied in a number of scuffles. Anne's father had picked up a short length of black-painted pipe after one of those fights, and he carried it jutting forward so that in the poor light it looked like the end of a sawed-off shotgun. Brian, after falling over the child's roller skate, had gotten up only to have a bat turn under his foot. This was small, but solid, and Brian had taken it along with him. Brian didn't know how he looked himself, but the dirtied face of Anne's father, lit by the red glow and with eyes in shadow, was not one to encourage troublemakers.

They were crossing the bridge over the river when Brian suddenly thought how calmly Cermak was taking it all. "I thought all this would be a terrible blow to you."

"So did I. Why, did Anne say something to you?"

"She said you foresaw it."

Cermak was quiet a moment, studying a car stalled just ahead. He shifted his length of pipe to cover it, and Brian dropped back a little, as if to give a clear field of fire.

Nothing moved in the car as they went past, but after-

48

wards Brian thought he heard a very faint creak of the springs. They both stiffened and turned. After a time they moved in closer. The car was deserted.

Cermak grunted. "What a stupid business this is. You get to suspect your own shadow." He clucked disapprovingly. "And people going around robbing others. For what? What does money mean now?" He glanced ahead, where all was clear to the bridge.

"Yes," he said, going back to the question Brian had asked him. "I *did* foresee it. But it's no credit to me. I just had a dream. I saw the lights go out, and the cars stop, and people rush out shouting, 'What's happened to the power?' I could see the whole thing, and when I woke up, I was near to being crazy. All my life I've worked underground, envying people who worked in the sunlight. Someone with more brains or better luck could have got out of the spot I was in. Until I was almost thirty, I never woke up to the fact that, first off, I was in the wrong part of the country, trying to get work where too many were out of a job. Then I had sense enough to get out of there. Twenty-nine years it took for this to dawn on me.

"All my life, I've been that way. Thrifty and hard-working, but stupid. The trouble is, it's not how hard you work that they pay you for, it's what you accomplish. A man could chip rock all his life with a sledge hammer, ten hours a day, and get less done in his whole life than another man could do in half an hour with a few sticks of dynamite. Which man deserves the more money? Another ten years it took me to see that. I was stupid, because I thought I could get ahead on hard work and always putting my money away, but finally it came to me a man has got to think, too. By then, I was in the rut it took me all those years to dig while I was being smart, working hard for pennies and putting the pennies in the savings bank. Finally it dawned on me that hard work was good, but you had to have hard thought, too. By this time it was a little late for me, but I could still help Anne. And it worked out. She had a good job, with good people. She could hold her head up. But a man still needs to work."

They crossed the street. No one bothered them.

THE DAY THE MACHINES STOPPED

Anne's father said, "It's hard to waste most of your life, finally see what's wrong, help your daughter to do things right, have things finally start to go right, and just then have everything smashed. I was almost ready to do away with myself this morning, but it dawned on me that that was wrong. Why do that when maybe my heart will finish me anyway? Besides, this awful thing at least has made people equal again. No one is going to be asking me how many grades I went in school. All those paper requirements don't mean a thing any more. I'm not happy about this mess, but somehow I feel useful again."

They went on in silence till they reached the Research East building. They climbed the stairs wearily to the fourth floor, found food, clothing, blankets, canteens, several .30-06 Springfield rifles, a box containing bandoliers of ammunition, and a map showing the route Cardan intended to follow. Brian copied the map, he and Cermak fell into exhausted sleep, and then, somewhat rested, they each took a canteen, rifle, a hundred and twenty rounds of ammunition, and as many supplies as they could pack on their backs, and went cautiously down to the street.

"Where now?" said Cermak. "Two thousand miles is a long trip on foot."

"Down the street and several blocks to the left, there's a bicycle shop. If Cardan gets held up getting fuel, or runs into a jam of cars and trucks, we may catch up yet."

They made their way to the shop, saw no bicycles in sight, but found several cartons containing partly assembled bikes. Half an hour later they had assembled two of them and were out of the city and on the highway. No one stopped them. Apparently, after the nightmarish day and night that had gone before, the city had fallen into a stupor of exhaustion. Brian was grateful that they wouldn't be there when it woke up.

Then he thought of Carl, riding comfortably down the road ahead.

A murderous anger gripped Brian, and he settled down to a steady, mile-eating pace.

Chapter 6

The highway stretched ahead of them, a long unending track reaching to the horizon, dotted with an endless succession of cars. Pedaling steadily, they went past dazed people torn loose from civilization and not yet drawn into any other pattern, drifting along uncertainly. Here and there they passed cars and trucks that had been pushed to one side, and occasionally they saw fresh signs of big truck tires to the side of the road, or on the grassy mall in the center. On the level or going downhill, they made good time. But going uphill was another matter. Brian estimated that they averaged about two miles an hour uphill, pushing the bicycles. This quickly became a serious matter.

The first day or two Brian and Steve Cermak traveled by day and slept at night, making use of the cars that were always nearby on the road. But as day followed day, the situation changed. Though the superhighway was designed to avoid passing directly through heavily populated cities, it often came close to them, leading Brian and Anne's father into clouds of smoke from burning cities, where the fire trucks couldn't run, the water pressure was down, and the firemen had to struggle like everyone else to save their own lives.

As the highway passed supermarkets and shopping centers, they saw rioting mobs, heard the crash of the big plate-glass windows, and the screams of trampled people. But out of this chaos, a new pattern began to emerge. Now they began to hear the sound of gunfire, saw men sprint from car to car, working their way along curbs and gutters and ditches, and race in small groups toward the sides and rear of chosen buildings. Now the battles were begining to rage for control of the stocks of food and manufactured goods. More and more often, the people they passed were armed, and the whine of bullets missing them narrowly warned them that they could easily join the bodies ever more thickly strewn along the road, lying motionless face-down, or on their backs, terrible eyes staring at the sky.

They crouched one day near a pine tree by the side of the road, hearing the bang and rattle of gunfire ahead, with the gloom of late afternoon deepened by heavy clouds of smoke, and lit by a towering pillar of flame rising from a large service station down the highway.

Cermak said, "We can't go on like this. Through these places, and when we're walking the bikes, it's too dangerous."

"We'd better keep out of sight by day, and travel at night," Brian said. He glanced at the road. "And right there is something else we'd better look out for."

Cermak followed his gaze, to look at the crouching figures bending over the prostrate bodies, briefly and expertly robbing them, then gliding on.

Cermak involuntarily raised his gun, then slowly lowered it.

Brian watched them warily. "Worse yet, there are traps and ambushes being set. That close call we had today was just a sample."

Brian and Cermak had been going downhill on the right side of the highway when Brian noticed the odd fact that, on both sides of the road, the lanes were blocked, the cars lined up almost abreast. Then he noticed another thing. In the right-hand lane, straight ahead, the front wheels of the car toward the side of the road were turned sharply to the left. If the car had been driving with the wheels in that position, it would have swung in front of the car to its left and been wrecked. Obviously, the car had been moved, steered downhill and parked in line with the other car. Brian glanced around. It was too late for him to brake. He leaned to his left, and the bike shot across the grass. Simultaneously, the door of a car to his right opened up and there was the loud report of a gun going off.

Brian glanced back, worried about Anne's father. There was no time for Brian to help him, but one quick glance was enough. Steve Cermak was forty feet behind, gripping the handle bars with his right hand, the big Springfield resting across his right forearm, his left hand gripping the small of the stock, and his left forefinger on the trigger. As Cermak passed the open door, he squeezed the trigger; there was a second, much louder, report, and that was the end of the trouble.

"Yes," said Cermak, looking down the road at the shopping plaza, where guns flashed in the twilight, and where the tall shadows of dark light poles wavered across the face of the buildings, lit by flames of fires burning out of control. "Yes, now honest people have the least chance, so we'll meet only human wolves, rats, and vultures." He looked at the shadowy figures flitting down the road from body to body, glanced around and gripped his gun tighter. Brian, too, unconsciously checked his gun, his thumb feeling to be sure the gun was cocked and the magazine cutoff turned up.

Brian and Cermak had suddenly become conscious that even if they escaped the other dangers, their food would soon run out. They were sparing it, and they still hoped to catch Cardan before they needed more. But their packs were lightening steadily.

In time they were away from the worst of the heavily populated districts, traveling through country that was almost wild in places, and very hilly. They still saw signs of the trucks that had gone before, and twice they had run into massive traffic jams that must have delayed Cardan and his men, but they hadn't caught up. Then, in a stretch of desolate country, they ran out of food, and there followed a day when their only refreshment was a drink from the canteens they filled at the numerous streams they passed.

The next day, while searching for food, they came to the third traffic jam. Here the pile-up of cars reached through a complicated cloverleaf at the base of a hill where a wide blacktopped road, also jammed with cars, passed under the superhighway. Farther down the superhighway, a line of toll gates stretched across the road. Huge signs told of a service station to the right, and food and lodging to the left. Down below, they could see people moving along past the cars, and disappearing under the overpass. Ahead, the cars were thick on the road, but on the other side, across the grass, where the cars had been leaving the toll gate, they were more spread out.

"Well?" said Cermak.

Brian shrugged. "We've got to have food."

"What about Cardan and your friend Carl?"

Brian drew a slow deep breath and checked their map. "That's it," he said. "They went down this ramp, and came up that one."

Off in the distance, to the left, there was a brief burst of gunfire. Cermak nodded. "There's food there—and trouble."

"Okay. Let's go, fast. If we want food, we can't avoid trouble."

They bent over the bikes, and, one behind the other, swooped down the hill, through the tollgates, and walked their bikes up a moderately steep hill.

They hid the bicycles in a kind of small oblong concrete room under the grassy center strip at the middle of a long culvert, the handle bars hooked through a set of bent pipes that made a ladder from a manhole overhead. They looked back in from outside, saw the bicycles were not conspicuous, and went on, taking only their empty packs, their guns, and a bandolier apiece of ammunition.

They climbed the bank by the road, pushed through the low trees, and found themselves in a soggy place where the water stood in thin puddles on gray muck, with the bare brush as thick as a hedge around them, and trees rising here and there, many of them dead, and reaching out before them into the distance.

It took several hours to get around this place, and by then the sun had climbed high overhead. But spread out below them, at the foot of a long gentle slope, was a shopping plaza.

Cermak grinned and nodded, then lost the grin as he studied the plaza.

The sound of gunfire was now loud and clear, and almost continuous. From amongst the cars jammed in the front of a parking lot, they could see an occasional dull flash, and many wisps of blowing smoke. Across the front and on both sides of the long block of buildings there seemed to be one continuous fight. Only to the rear was there no sign of fighting. There, sawhorses blocked off the parking lot where some repair work was being done on a drainage system. Just beyond the line of sawhorses, there was a long ditch, and nearby, several bodies stretched out awkwardly, where they had tried to make it around the side to the rear, and failed.

Cermak said, "They're coming from both directions along that road. See there?"

From along the road to the right, Brian could see a slow trickling of armed men, hidden from the buildings by the lines of cars.

Brian watched intently. "They work in close to the front of the buildings, by the cars in that lot. If they leave the cars, they've got a hundred feet of dirt and asphalt to cross, and a ditch, before they get around in back."

"You see those little holes knocked in the side, high up in that blank wall back of the show window?" Cermak asked.

"Yes," Brian said, his eyes pinpointing on the occasional flashes appearing at these holes. "Yes, I see. They can shoot across the lot and straight into the ditch from there."

"It's a deathtrap," Cermak said. "But from down there, you wouldn't know it till it was too late."

"I wonder if anyone's watching the back."

The two men studied the apparently bare dirt at the back of the plaza. On closer examination, it looked like blacktop tracked over with dirt from the excavation. There was a drainage ditch around the lot, and beyond that, empty fields. To one side, the ditch ran back straight across the foot of the slope where Brian and Cermak looked out from behind a screen of thick brush. From where they sat in relation to this ditch, there was scattered cover. From the ditch to the rear of the stores there wasn't enough cover to hide a mouse.

They studied the buildings carefully. Cermak cleared his throat. "They should have someone covering the rear. But there's a lot of shooting down there."

"They could be hard pressed."

There was a moment's silence as they looked over the bare fields to either side. No one down there was trying to get

55

across those bare fields to the rear. Everyone was coming along the road, where the jammed cars offered cover.

Again they studied the empty parking lot at the rear, the ditches leading to it, and the empty space that had to be crossed to get to the back door.

Finally Cermak said, "Well, I've seen bear traps I'd rather walk into than this thing. But if we don't go down there, what do we eat?"

Carefully, stealthily, they eased down the slope toward the ditch.

It seemed to take them forever as they worked their way along the slippery, steep-banked ditch with the sucking-mud bottom under slow-flowing icy water, then they were peering out through the dead grass at the stretch of dusty, empty parking lot at the rear of the stores. They lay still there for long minutes, studying the doors, ventilators, trash cans, and the cement-block wall of the building.

Not moving, Cermak murmured, "See anything?"

"Not a thing." Brian very carefully tilted his head sidewise to study the roof, then slowly and carefully glanced around to either side.

"Funny nobody at all tries to get around this way."

"They've got wide-open fields on either side. There's no cover. But it stands to reason they ought to have a guard inside, watching this way, just in case."

"I don't see any."

"I don't either."

Brian was looking at the vacant parking lot. He'd seen empty spaces in his life, but nothing that compared with this. From his low ground-level viewpoint, it appeared to stretch out, flat and bare, for a hundred yards in front of them.

Cermak laughed suddenly. "Looks like a damned airfield, doesn't it? Well, if we wait, someone else may get the same idea. Ready?"

Brian braced himself. "Ready as I'll ever be."

Cermak's voice was low and hoarse. "We'll head for the red door of that supermarket. When I count three. One—two—"

Brian cautiously eased himself a little farther up the bank. "Three," said Cermak.

They scrambled up the bank and sprinted across the parking lot.

Brian was pumping his legs as fast as they could go, but he had the feeling of crossing a mile-wide mud flat at a leisurely crawl.

Then abruptly the cement-block wall at the rear of the building was right in front of him, and slowing down was just as hard as running had been. He whirled at the last minute to lightly bang the wall with his upper arms and back, and looked quickly around, the gun raised. But no guard was in sight on the roof of the building. He took hold of the red-painted door and, a moment later, he and Cermak were in a bare whitewashed room with a few empty crates on the floor. They went through an open door to one side, and found themselves in a room about twenty feet wide, apparently running the full depth of the store, with boxes and cardboard cartons stacked from one end to the other.

At the far end of the room, high up, was a small irregular patch of light, where someone looked out and fired. No one else was in sight, but the firing from the front of the store was rising to a crescendo.

Using their pocketknives, they tore open nearby cartons, finding baby food, big jars of pickles, mustard, relish, bottles of ketchup—all the things they didn't care to find themselves living on for the next week. Warily, they eased up the aisle, in clear view of the man at the hole, if he merely turned around. They reached a pair of swinging doors with small diamond-shaped windows and Brian cautiously glanced out. A barricade of food cartons, bales of garden mulch, and overturned shooping carts blocked the aisles where the row of checkout counters faced the long, smashed front window of the store. Behind the barricade, men crouched and fired in a haze of smoke, while outside in the parking lot, a row of cars rolled forward slowly, the front wheels climbing over the outstretched bodies that lay here in the smashed glass.

Behind the cars, there had to be people pushing, and when the cars reached the front of the building, then it would be possible for them to gather in numbers, right next to the building, for one final rush.

Cermak quickly loaded Brian's pack. The cars were coming steadily on, almost to the curb, and now one of the men in the store glanced back nervously over his shoulder.

Brian loaded Cermak's pack, his fingers feeling thick and clumsy, and fastened down the flap. They went quickly down the aisle, then something *whanged* over Brian's head as he turned, and a stinging shower of bits of cement hit him on the side of the face. Then they were at the back door. On the other side was that stretch of parking lot, and Brian could see its empty flat bareness from the doorway. Behind them, the firing rose to a new height, and now there were yells, curses, and the pound of feet.

"Come on," Cermak whispered. He threw the door back and they bolted onto the lot.

This time fast motion was more difficult than before. The goods in Brian's pack bounced around as he ran, the pack itself bounced on its frame, the frame started to shift as a fastening loosened, and the lot seemed to stretch out forever. When they were halfway across, something whined past Brian's head, and an instant later there was a puff of dust ahead and a black groove appeared, showing the asphalt through the accumulated dirt.

Something plucked lightly at Brian's pack, what sounded like a swarm of yellow jackets whined past overhead, and then the ditch was at his feet. Brian hit the opposite bank of it hard, slid, and landed calf-deep in the icy slop and ooze.

Cermak was in the same situation to Brian's left. "Keep low," he muttered, and began working his way along the bank. Brian followed.

Behind them, the firing was intense and continuous.

It had taken them a long time to get to the shopping plaza along the ditch and, because of their load, it took them longer to get back. At intervals, bullets whined overhead, and when they finally scrambled thankfully up the bank through the brush on the hill overlooking the shopping plaza, they were worn out. They took a look back, eying the bodies strewn over the lot in the rear of the supermarket.

There was still an almost continuous firing, but Brian, looking down, was unable to see who was fighting whom.

Cermak said, "We got out of there just in time. We were lucky, but it isn't over yet."

They paused to eat the first food they'd had in a day and a half, then wearily made their way around the swampy stretch and back down toward where they'd hidden the bikes.

They'd scarcely gotten the bikes out when there was a rattle of gunfire, increasing in intensity and then gradually dying away again.

"Better get going," said Brian. "We can sleep when we put this place well behind us."

They coasted down the hill. Brian was just beginning to breathe easily as the bike glided swiftly ahead, when there was the faint dull glint of something stretched across the road, then the bike twisted and slid fast to the right, spilling him to land heavily on the pavement.

A dark figure scrambled out of the ditch, there was the flash of an upraised knife, and a deafening roar as Cermak fired across Brian's shoulder.

An instant later Brian had his own gun unslung and was firing at a dim figure that raced toward them from a nearby car. Then Brian and Cermak were working their bolts as rapidly as possible, and the shadowy figures were coming at them from all sides, outlined now in a white light that rose over the hill.

Brian's bolt stuck wide-open, warning him that the magazine was empty, and he knew he had no time to reload. He waited, the gun muzzle drawn back, ready to slam into the chest of the first attacker to come in reach.

Then two of these attackers spun around and slammed to the earth, and the rest ran down the hill to stagger in midstride and fall.

A blinding glare moved down the road and, through the ringing in his ears, Brian could hear Cardan's roar, "Stop the trucks! Those men are ours!"

At the sound of Cardan's voice, Brian walked to the cab of the truck. Cermak, frowning, stepped to the side of the road.

Then the big trucks were stopped, and Cardan, a .45 automatic in his right hand, jumped out, grinned, gripped Brian by the left hand, turned, and shouted, "Shove those cars out of the way! Scouts out! And make sure of these bodies here!" He looked at Brian and smiled. "You not only caught up—you got ahead of us. Are you all right?"

"By the grace of God," said Brian fervently. "Another minute would have been too late."

"That's all it takes." Cardan turned away to answer the shouted question of a man who came running over, and then Brian saw someone else.

The athletic build and blond hair were familiar, and so was the intent, calculating expression.

And then Carl sauntered toward the two men.

Chapter 7

Brian looked at Carl's clean-shaven, well-rested face. He appeared to be in good shape, looking as if he'd been sleeping at night and eating regularly in the daytime. Moreover, he appeared to know it. His head was tilted slightly, with something of the look of superiority with which the son of a wealthy man might look at the sweaty child of a ditchdigger.

Beside Cardan, someone said, "Chief, there's quite a roadblock up ahead. The cars are too close to get by, and they're clear across the mall in the center. This gang here must have set it up so that no-one could rush them and get away."

"Clear it out," said Cardan. "Keep your eyes open, and use the chains. It may be like that setup we ran into the first time we stopped for fuel."

"We'll be careful."

Cardan glanced at Brian. "It's good to have you back."

He smiled suddenly. "Here's someone else who feels the same way."

Anne, her blond hair brushed and shining in the light of the gasoline lanterns, started to run to Brian, and caught herself at the last moment, a mixture of emotions struggling on her face.

"Oh, Brian," she said at last, smiling happily, "I'm so glad you're here!" She frowned. "But why did you—?"

Carl's voice cut in. "We've found your father, Anne."

Anne turned, to cry out, like a child, "Daddy!"

She ran to the elder Cermak, who, unnecessarily steadied by one of Cardan's men, was coming toward them, his Springfield rifle gripped firmly in his right hand. Cermak smiled as he saw Anne, but his eyes narrowed intently when he looked at Carl.

Carl stood about six feet from Brian, a look of satisfaction on his face. A little louder than was necessary, Carl said, "Decide you couldn't make it on your own, Brian?"

Through a layer of gathering weariness from the hundreds of miles covered on the bicycle, lack of sleep and food, and the two narrow escapes of the day, Brian became aware of an ugly sensation, deep down inside himself. He remembered Carl's footsteps behind him, the blow on the back of the head. Out of the corner of his eye, Brian could see several of the men watching him and Carl.

Cermak had returned his daughter's kiss, and now spoke briefly to her. She shook her head. Cermak spoke more forcibly, and then thrust her aside. He jerked open the bolt of his rifle; an empty cartridge flashed in the light as it flew out, then in one blur of motion Cermak stuffed a fresh clip into the magazine and slammed home the bolt. He watched Brian and Carl without expression.

Carl was looking down at Brian. "Afraid to speak?"

Brian was aware of a steady dull ache in his left arm, where he had landed when the bike overturned, a slow throb at the back of his neck, and a multitude of aches and stiffnesses, all felt through a haze of weariness. Something told Brian that his chance of beating Carl now was nonexistent. The only thing to do was to put off the fight till he had some rest. But how?"

61

Carl's eyes glinted. "You don't look very good, Brian. You'd have done better to come with us in the first place."

No one else said anything. But it became obvious to Brian, despite his weariness, that Carl was speaking for the benefit of the others.

Carl said, "I don't like a guy that runs out. You're here now, and I suppose we'll have to take care of you, but I think you need a lesson."

From several of the men watching came an approving murmur.

Carl stepped forward. There was a flash, a deafening roar, and the pungent smell of burned nitrocellulose. Something lightly ruffled Carl's hair.

There was a dead silence for an instant after the shot, and then Carl very slowly turned his head.

Cermak handed his gun to his daughter, and grinned at Carl.

"Fight *me*, why don't you?"

Carl blinked.

"Daddy!" cried Anne.

"No, no," said Cermak, holding her back with one hand. "He's tough. He and Brian go off together and only Carl comes back. Carl tells his story, and Brian isn't there, so of course only one side gets told. Carl's side. Then Carl rides along protected by everyone else, while Brian has to fight his way for hundreds of miles, on his own muscle. After he's worn out, Big Carl shows up riding in a truck and he's going to teach Brian a lesson for being so cowardly as to fight his way across hundreds of miles of territory, by himself, with an old man to lug on his back. This Carl is a big fellow. If someone else does something brave, that makes Carl a hero."

There was a motionless stillness in which the hiss and roar of the gas lanterns sounded loud and clear, and all the men in sight were frowning at Carl and glancing in puzzlement from Carl to Brian to Anne's father.

Brian kept his face from showing the grin he felt at Cermak's sarcasm. The only flaw in the argument was that Carl, from what Brian had seen, was no coward. He would lie and misrepresent whenever it suited his advantage, but

Brian had seen no sign of cowardice. The men who were with Carl must have had time to find this out by now.

"Oh," said Carl, a look of relief crossing his face as he saw a way out. "I forgot he's had time to fill you full of lies."

He turned to face Brian, a look of genuine anger on his face. It was anger at the spot he found himself in. "You'd stoop to anything, wouldn't you?" He glanced at Anne. "Take care of your father, Anne. He's tired, and this rat has been pumping him full of lies. And keep that gun away from him. We can't have anyone around who shoots at his friends."

He glanced at Brian. "Don't have much to say for yourself, do you?" He glanced to one side, saw that several men were holding the smiling Cermak, and immediately took one long step forward, reaching out a big hand and knocked loose the gun Brian had been absently holding since the trucks had shown up.

Brian still stood unmoving, the accumulated fatigue combining with the unfairness of the attack to create a feeling of unreality, as if he were watching someone else rather than experiencing it himself.

"This," said Carl, "is for running out on me." His open hand struck Brian jarringly across the side of the head. His other hand slapped Brian's face in a stinging explosion from the other side. "And *that's* for telling my girl's father lies."

Carl landed a lightning blow to the stomach that left Brian gasping, and then Carl had him by the cloth at the throat, holding him up as he said, "I don't like to do it, Brian, but you've got to learn if you're going with us. You don't leave your friends to do all the work. And you don't lie about it afterwards. *You hear me?*"

From somewhere to the side, Cermak's voice reached them.

"You tell him, Carl hero. You've had the sleep."

There was a murmur that might have meant anything, but Brian, out on his feet before Carl had ever touched him, felt Carl's hand tighten and lift brutally.

For one blinding instant, Brian saw himself held like a

63

rag doll while Carl taunted him, hoping for Brian to struggle a little, giving Carl further excuse to slap him around.

Brian was suddenly wide-awake. He let go a crushing blow to Carl's jaw, and saw him stagger back. He caught up with him in three swift steps, yanked him upright, and struck him a blow that came up from the ground. An instant later, Brian's open left hand lashed out twice, repaying the slaps in the face, then his right buried itself deep in Carl's midsection, doubling Carl up as if he'd been hit with a telephone pole.

Carl was on the ground, his eyes glazed, and Brian was standing over him, his mind running back through the things Carl had said and done, aching for the justification to land one more blow, but vaguely aware that the accounts had been evened up and anything more would place the discredit on his side.

Then the anger was gone, and he was breathing hard, aware of a dizziness and a tiredness, of the pain in his left arm, and of aches, stiffnesses, sore muscles, and a throbbing head.

Men were crowded around and someone was shouting for water. Someone gripped Brian's shoulder, and he turned to see Steve Cermak, grinning broadly.

"That punk has been filling Anne with lies." He glanced at the prostrate Carl; a bucket of water was being emptied in his face. "I never saw anything so pretty in my life. Come on."

They started toward the trucks, then Brian remembered the gun Carl had knocked from his hands, found it, carried the gun toward the truck that someone pointed out as a place where he and Cermak could sleep, and then he remembered the bicycles. With someone else carrying a gas lantern, they found the bikes, one smashed out of shape and the other perfectly usable, and put them in the truck. With these safely on board, they crawled into the roomy interior, and found places to settle down in the soft hay.

After a long, dreamless sleep, Brian stirred to the rumble of the truck. Daylight was seeping in around the door at the far end. But it was warm nestled in the soft hay, and

Brian drifted off to sleep again. He woke the next time with someone gently shaking his shoulder. Light was streaming in at the open back of the truck, and Brian woke, stretched, winced at his swollen knuckles, and scrambled to his feet.

Smitty, clean-shaven, grinned at Brian.

"I let you sleep through breakfast, but I figured you'd want lunch. There's a stream back in the trees to the right of the road if you want to wash up. The cook-truck has hot water, soap, and some mirrors for shaving. You can take your time. We're broken down again."

"What's wrong?"

"The usual. Apparently when the binding of the electrons to the metal atoms was increased it wasn't only the conduction of the electricity that suffered. Brightness and *heat* conductivity are off, too. The metal of the pistons and cylinders in the engines doesn't get cooled as well as it should; it overheats, and just what goes on in there is hard to say, but we've had cracked blocks, pitting, spalling off of bits of metal, pistons stuck tight in the cylinders. I don't know what it is this time, but we were due for it. We get a breakdown every few hundred miles. At least it didn't happen at night."

Brian followed Smitty past a number of bed rolls he hadn't noticed the night before, and dropped out of the truck.

"Hard to work on at night?" asked Brian.

"Unless you've already cleaned out the place, you don't know who's going to take a pot shot at you. Moreover, if a truck stops all of a sudden, there's a chance of two trucks slamming into each other. In the daytime, we run further apart."

"At night, it's dangerous to get separated?"

Smitty nodded. "The highway is bad enough, but when you go off it to get fuel, food, or anything else, all hell breaks loose. Either some bunch of thugs has already grabbed what you want, or else there's a vigilance committee, citizens' protective association, or something just as good, right there to see the thugs *don't* grab the place. Either way, you're an outsider, and they don't want you.

Then there're setups like what you ran into last night. If you hadn't set them off first, they'd have hit us later when we stopped to get the roadblock out of the way. *They* wait for somebody to rob a place like that shopping center, then they, in turn, ambush the robbers."

"Nice," said Brian ironically.

"Isn't it? The trouble is, everybody has to eat."

They were walking along past the trucks, and Smitty said, "Here's the cook-truck. 'Morning, Barbara, Anne.'"

Anne Cermak and Barbara Bowen smiled at Smitty, and then at Brian. Brian was suddenly conscious of his dirty clothes and unshaven face. But he was also hungry. There was a large kettle of stew cooking slowly on a bottled-gas stove inside the truck, and a pile of bowls of unbreakable plastic, and a tray of stainless-steel spoons.

Brian took a bowl of stew off to one side, ate hungrily, then went off to the stream to wash up. He came back shaved, and by now the small, cursing crowd at the front of one of the trucks had subsided, the hood was down again, the women and children on the grass at the center of the road were going back to the trucks, and the men were coming out of the woods and back from up and down the road where they'd been serving as guards and lookouts.

Brian hunted up Cardan, who put him on one of the trucks as a guard. Anne's father volunteered as the driver, but Anne herself was in another truck with Barbara Bowen.

The days passed pleasantly enough—by comparison with what it had been like when Brian and Cermak were traveling by bicycle—but Brian couldn't help noticing that every day the going got tougher.

The cars were getting thicker along the roads, which meant many more obstacles to go around, or to get them out of the way. The trucks were already carrying a number of cans of extra fuel, which they stopped to refill at every opportunity. But they were low on food, and as Cardan was determined to get more before they ran out, the result was a carefully planned raid on a shopping center. This took an entire day, and was immediately followed by an ambush worse than any they'd run into before.

Brian had looked forward to being with Anne, but they

were in separate trucks while traveling, and when they were stopped there was a desperate need for guards and lookouts.

At every stop Cardan now had some of the men bolting tight more big oblongs of the galvanized iron roofing he'd loaded up with after the last raid on a shopping center, and which now, in several layers of thickness, served to armor the trucks against the fire of most light hand-weapons. The extra protection was needed, since they were now being fired on by people who apparently shot for fun as well as plunder. They were getting into a section like a suburb of hell. Cars and trucks were burnt out, the roads were strewn with broken bottles, barbed wire, and spike-studded boards; the ditches were dug into trench systems, and an explosion had knocked out a wide section of overpass. From all sides there was continuous firing, with leaping flames devouring the buildings in the background, and a pall of smoke blotting out what lay beyond. Cardan pulled back out of it, sent the steam car on a brief reconnaissance to the south, learned that it was no better that way, tried a wider detour, and ran into another mess. Before they were through, they'd gone a hundred miles out of their way, suffered painful wounds, and repaired half a dozen tires. It took the better part of a week to get back on the highway.

"Well," said Smitty, studying a map, "I think that was Cleveland. One of these days, if we last long enough, we'll hit Chicago. I'm not looking forward to it."

Once again they were making good time. They were well stocked with provisions, and at every stop the men were strengthening the protection of the trucks. Now more of the rear tires were shielded, and metal disks were fitted to the front wheels. Small-caliber bullets striking from the side would do little damage unless very well aimed. "But," as Cardan pointed out, "a few gasoline bombs heaved at us out of a ditch could end the whole thing." He decided on a wide detour to avoid Chicago, at the same time staying well north of Indianapolis. By now, no city looked attractive to them.

Several days later they seemed to be in the clear again, traveling along a wide, deserted road, weaving occasionally to pass the inevitable cars, when Brian, traveling this time in the steam car that raced in front of the trucks to see what was up ahead, saw a cloud of dust far ahead as they swooped over a low rise.

"Now," said Brian, pointing out the dust cloud, "what do you suppose makes that?"

"Either a lot of animals," said Cermak, frowning, "or a lot of people."

Smitty, driving, said, "Whichever it is, that's a sizable migration."

He slowed the steam car. They studied the dust cloud for a moment, then they raced ahead for a closer look.

Cermak cleared his throat. "If that's a migration, it's got a leader. If he's got any sense, he'll have flank guards watching this road."

Smitty slowed to a stop. Ahead and to either side was a gentle rise covered on the left with small trees now starting to leaf out. Most of the rest of the land they'd passed was open farm country, the fields already plowed and ready to be planted by the tractors that no longer ran.

Smitty swung the car around and they reported back to Cardan, who nodded thoughtfully. "We'll keep going, but stop short of that place. From what you say, they're headed south, and we're going west. We'll wait till the column, whatever it is, goes past."

A little while later they were there, the head of the dust cloud now perceptibly further to the south. But the tail of the cloud was still out of sight to the north.

"If," Smitty suggested, "we could get through those woods beside the road, we could look down on whatever it is that's going past on the other side."

"Go ahead," said Cardan. "But be careful. This is a bad setup, and there's no telling what you may run into."

Smitty, Brian and Steve Cermak walked up into the woods. It was a cool day, but the ground was soft underfoot, and the small leaves just coming out gave the forest a misty, delicate appearance. The sky overhead was a clear blue, with only a few high clouds. There was a light breeze, and it carried the sound of voices.

Then Brian was near the edge of a low steep bank, looking down through the trees, seeing, on a wide dirt road below, a column of men.

Brian glanced back over his shoulders to where Smitty and Cermak, further back in amongst the trees, covered him from either side.

As he turned to look back, he saw, about forty feet away, three men standing in the shadow of a tall evergreen. They were watching him, their guns not quite aimed at him, but requiring only a slight shift to be centered on him. One of them called out in a low voice. "What you doing, man?"

"Looking," said Brian, all his senses alert.

"You alone?"

"My friends are covering me."

"We don't see them."

"They'd be careless if you did."

"What you planning?"

"We wanted to go past. But we can wait."

"Which way you headed?"

"West."

"And you're sure your friends have got us covered?" the man asked slyly.

"Make a false move, and you'll find out," Brian said amiably.

"How many of them?" the man wanted to know.

"Only a dozen," said Brian, "but all good shots."

The man hesitated, his gun hand itching to swing his weapon around. For a moment there was a deathly silence as uncertainty plagued the man. Abruptly he relaxed, grinned from ear to ear, let out a bellow of a laugh, and commented, "I believe you."

Almost nonchalantly, he motioned to his companions and they took off to join their column. Brian heaved a deep sigh of relief and walked back to where Smitty and Cermak were waiting.

"What was all that about?" asked Cermak.

"I tried a bluff," Brian said. "And it worked. But for a moment there it was touch and go." He wiped the perspiration off his forehead.

Their release from extreme tension made them feel almost hilarious, and Smitty and Cermak congratulated Brian on his handling of the situation.

"Well," said Brian, "I couldn't have pulled it off if you

two weren't there to back me up. How were they to know whether there were two of you or a dozen?"

Sudden gunfire erupted in the direction where they had left the trucks. Obviously, they weren't in the clear yet.

As one, they moved through the woods toward the firing. Long before they got back, the gunfire had ended.

Chapter 8

Brian, Smitty and Cermak looked cautiously on one burning truck. The other trucks and the steam car were gone. On the road lay one of Cardan's men, a long hunting arrow jutting from his back. On a hill nearby was another man dead, an arrow embedded in the base of his neck. A dead stranger, still holding a bow and a quiver of hunting arrows had been shot through the chest.

Anne, smeared with mud and dirt, climbed from a ditch by the side of the road. She explained that Cardan had been talking to her when the trouble started, and he had thrown her down out of sight and told her to crawl into a nearby culvert. There she had heard the fight, but had seen nothing of what happened.

As they were trying to reconstruct what had taken place, Carl, fully dressed, his hair wet, and unarmed save for the knife at his belt, walked down the gentle, sparsely wooded slope on the opposite side of the road, carrying a towel in one hand. He had a sick weary look, and for once paid no attention to Anne.

Brian and others waited silently. Carl walked over, drew a ragged breath, and looked at them steadily.

"I saw it all," he said dazedly. "And I couldn't do a thing."

There was a silence, and Brian said, "Where were you?"

"Up the slope, washing in the stream. The scouts checked

the woods on both sides and sent word that everything was all clear. Cardan didn't like the spot, but finally let the women and kids get out for some air. I felt sweaty and dirty because I'd been on guard at that last place and didn't have a chance to wash. I found a stream, followed it uphill, and didn't bother to take my gun because I wasn't going far. The stream wound across this open field, and I had to go way up to find a place that was out of sight. I'd no sooner started to wash than there was the bang of Cardan's .45, and there went our two guards on this side, running down the hill. The thing was over before I could do anything. About a dozen guys in camouflage suits, armed with bows and arrows, came out of the woods across the road, covered the women and children, made the men start up the trucks, and took off. They apparently knocked over a portable stove Barbara Bowen had lit to heat some coffee, and that set one truck on fire. They took the rest of the trucks and the steam car."

They looked at him silently, seeing the attack in their minds.

Carl took the silence for censure, and said almost pleadingly, "I couldn't do a thing. When they left, I made it up to the top of the slope to the east there, saw them turn off onto a dirt road headed north. That's all I know."

Smitty, finally said, "Did they kill Cardan?"

"I don't think so. But I think he got one of them."

"Then they'll regret this—if they live long enough."

Cermak was frowning. "Where did they come from? What were they doing here?"

Brian said, "They could have planned to attack that column we ran into, decided it was too much, turned back this way and heard the children. The guards could have been watching the other way at the wrong moment, and those arrows would have made no sound that would warn people down here."

Smitty looked around at the desolate scene. "I wish the chief had had one of his hunches about this."

"Maybe he did," said Carl. "Miss Bowen had to beg him to let the women and kids get out of the trucks."

"If the woods and the road had already been checked, and there were guards watching, what did he see he didn't like?" asked Cermak.

"The chief works on hunches more than you'd think," Smitty informed them. "It sounds crazy, but when you get right down to it, he's *got* to. He's used to dealing with things that aren't known well enough yet to handle precisely. I think what he sees is the sum total of a whole lot of things, each too small to mean much by itself. When he's uneasy like that, there's generally a reason."

Carl said, "Like the dream he had before all this started. He was in a terrible mood, and we thought it was all for nothing. *Now* look."

Cermak said, "He had a dream?"

Smitty nodded. "He didn't exactly foresee what would happen. He was just uneasy about the general trend in certain kinds of research. And he was right."

They stood still for a minute, looking around and wondering what to do now.

Brian glanced at Carl. "One of the scouts is on that hill back there, dead. His gun is still with him. And there's one of their men, with a bow and some arrows."

Carl nodded his head in thanks, crossed the road, and climbed up the bank into the woods and out of sight.

Smitty watched him go. "He seems to be telling the truth. But I'm not enthusiastic about having him with us."

Cermak checked his gun. "I'd trust him as far as I could spit a mouthful of fishhooks."

Brian had given little heed to Carl since their fight, but now he thought the situation over carefully. "I think he'll be all right—provided we keep our eyes open if we get in a spot where it would pay him to stab us in the back."

Cermak cradled his gun. "It's never going to pay him to stab us in the back." He said to his daughter, "If he talks to you about going off with him or anything like that, let us know." He turned to Brian. "If he's going with us, Anne had better stick with me. The more Carl sees you and Anne together, the more likely we are to have trouble."

Brian agreed, but he was galled at the realization that once again Carl was keeping Brian and Anne apart.

Across the road, Carl slid down the hill, the bow and quiver slung across his back, a bandolier of ammunition over his shoulder, a rifle in his hand.

That night, they camped near where the trucks had been. The night was cold, they had no blankets, didn't want to show a fire, and woke early feeling cramped and stiff. And now they had no food. Since there was nothing else to do, they started walking. They kept going to the west, hoping to find some farm where they might get food.

Early that morning they found a farm, but a fusillade of shots greeted them when they got near it. They walked on. The same thing happened at the next farm. The third time it happened, Smitty shouted, "We want to buy food!"

A bullet screamed close overhead in answer.

They lay on the ground studying the building. It was a two-story frame structure, with one bare tree about forty feet from it on the far side. Save for the ruins of a burned-down barn, and shrubs to either side of the front door, there was no cover, and the land all around was flat.

Brian shouted, "Trade you bullets for food!"

There was a silence, then a deep male shout. "What size gun?"

"Springfield thirty."

"Wrong size!"

There was a moment's quiet, then a shouted warning, "Don't come any closer! We'll shoot to kill! We've been burnt out once and we're taking no chances!"

Brian looked at the blackened ruins of the barn.

He shouted, "Know any place we could get food?"

"Can't tell you. Everybody's in the same spot we're in."

Cermak growled, "I see his point. But I'm still hungry."

Brian lay flat, and said in a low voice, "How many guns fired at us that first time?"

"I'd say there were at least three of them," Carl volunteered. "Two downstairs, and I think there was a flash from that upstairs window to the left of the door."

Smitty said, "Better clear out. We haven't got any advantage, and it might just occur to them to shoot us and have our guns and bullets for themselves."

Brian called, "Thanks, anyway."

"Sorry we can't help you. Could give you water."

"Thanks. We've got that." Brian glanced around. "Let's get out of here."

Carl said, "One at a time. We'd better cover each other on the way."

They got away from the house without trouble, though when it was clear that they were leaving, the people at the house started calling questions as to what conditions were like along the road, when they'd eaten last, and whether they were sure they had plenty of water.

Smitty said, looking back, "Well, they *wanted* to help."

"There's not many calories in that," Carl commented wryly. "And we'll probably get the same business at the next place."

Toward noon, they reached another farmhouse, and except for a different voice, their greeting was the same. The people would have liked to help them, but they couldn't.

Later Brian and the others halted as another farmhouse, a two-story frame structure like the others, came into sight.

Cermak said dryly, "We could get very hungry this way."

"Well," said Brian, "let's think it over. We've got four guns, plenty of bullets, a bow, arrows, and a quiver. We need food, blankets, and it wouldn't hurt if we had a pack to carry more food in. Is that right?"

"That about covers it," said Smitty.

"Okay," said Brian. "With this much firepower, we ought to be able either to trade something for food, or else make it worth somebody's while to at least give us enough to get on to the next place."

"Now we're talking," Cermak said. "A bullet from one of our guns would probably go right through these houses, from one side to the other."

"Only," said Smitty, "it might kill somebody on the way. Say there's a man, wife, and three sons in one of those houses. The men are armed, and we accidentally shoot the mother. Not only does that make us murderers, but very shortly we're going to have something on our hands that won't be easy to end."

Brian said, "Why don't we be reasonable, like we have been, only this time insist on something to keep us going to the next place where they might have food. They ought to be able to spare us that much. If they won't, we could offer to trade, maybe, one gun and bullets, or the bow and arrows, for food, blankets and something to carry things in. If that doesn't work, we could warn them we'd fight, and give them a demonstration."

."If they wanted to trade for the bow and arrows, all right." Cermak agreed grudgingly, "but we may need every bullet and gun we've got."

Carl said, "In time, this bow is going to be worth much more than it's worth now. You can make your own arrows, with practice. And after you shoot them, you can go get them and shoot them again. Once we run out of bullets, the guns will be useless."

Smitty said, "Let's go to that next farmhouse and see what happens."

This time, after they'd made a careful reconnaissance and crept up by way of the barn and outbuildings, the house turned out to be empty. The livestock was gone, most of the cooking utensils and part of the bedding were gone, and in the cellar were wide shelves where rings in the dust showed that many dozens of jars of canned goods had been removed. There remained a few odd jars of vegetables, pickles and fruit, dated several years before. In the pantry that adjoined the kitchen were a few potatoes and onions, and a large box of oatmeal.

While Anne did the best she could to turn this into a meal, the men made up blanket rolls. Late that afternoon they were on the move again, fortified with boiled potatoes and onions, bread-and-butter pickles, and stewed tomatoes, followed by a dessert of canned peaches. With them they carried the bedrolls, a few pans, and the box of oatmeal. They wore improvised packs, and as the cloth straps dug into their shoulders, they wished they had never thought of that idea.

The next farm they passed was a large one, where men were working in the fields with horse-drawn, seed-sowing machines. Brian, Anne and the others were scarcely in sight when the bullets began to fly over their heads.

This became a pattern they gradually got used to. A few

isolated farms, held by small groups of people; other farms abandoned. At the abandoned farms there were usually some odd scraps of food to be found, and the buildings provided shelter. But there was seldom enough food, and often they had to sleep out during cold, wet, miserable nights.

Brian was aware that as the days passed they were gradually getting weaker. Worse yet, they were now well into a section of the country that had been visited by too many outsiders and didn't care to see more. Many of the farms were completely burned out. The people in those that still stood didn't talk, but opened fire on sight. The larger farms resorted to more drastic action, and parties of men charged out on horseback, only to hurriedly change their minds when the long-range accuracy of the four Springfields began picking off horses and men before they could get close.

Brian and the others found themselves near a small town where, they felt, there must be supplies, but the occasional sound of guns from the town made their approach cautious, and the sight of lone figures sprinting from one building to another amidst a fusillade of shots changed their minds entirely.

Smitty shook his head. "The whole country's gone crazy."

Cermak shrugged. "They've got to eat."

Carl said wearily, "It's the same thing as back home: no power, no lights, no communications, no transport. The country was run on electricity and now that's gone."

To the northeast, and far off to the south, Brian could see pillars of smoke. From somewhere toward the southwest came the sound of continuous gunfire, clearly audible now that the shots from the nearby town had died away. Wherever there was any sign of people, there was trouble in one form or another. The convulsion was coming to a climax, and Brian knew the motivation. As Cermak had said, people had to eat.

The next day, from a low hill, they looked off to the south on a moderately large shopping center. From the tall dead electric sign over the center, snipers were picking off the attackers who crept toward them through the flat fields nearby. Cars had been rolled off the roads leading to the center and burned. At the center itself, the cars in the parking lot had been pushed into a tight circle around the buildings, and the air let out of the tires so that no one could crawl underneath. From behind the cars, the defenders had a clear field of fire at anyone trying to cross the wide sweep of parking lot, where the only cover was the isolated light poles, dominated by the huge electric sign overhead. Plainly enough, the people outside couldn't get at the food without killing the defenders, while the people inside couldn't keep the food without killing whoever tried to force his way in. Meanwhile, the people inside would have no reliable way to get water. It looked bad enough in the daytime, but what neither Brian nor the others could visualize was what happened on a dark night when no one could tell friend from foe, and hungry men and women crept desperately across the parking lot, knives and guns in hand, toward the buildings.

As they looked at the building, it began to come home to them.

Smitty cleared his throat. "Let's move on."

One afternoon, tired, hungry and sick of the endless burning, looting and killing, Brian and the others lay down to rest in a clump of trees near a narrow blacktopped road by a stream. It was still broad daylight, and after they had rested they hoped to go on several miles more before nightfall.

They had scarcely begun to settle down when there was the bang of guns close by.

Chapter 9

Brian sprang to his feet and worked his way carefully through the trees. In a moment he was peering out at a stream where several farmers were guiding two teams of rearing horses as they drew wagons through the water toward a narrow blacktopped road. From a patch of brush atop a nearby embankment there came the flash of guns.

After what he had seen in the last few weeks, the situation was crystal clear at a glance. Brian took a quick look at the farmers, their honest, hard-working faces twisted in despair, then he dropped behind a thick log and slammed roaring shot after shot into the brush. As he stripped a fresh clip into the magazine, he shouted, "Carl! Smitty! Steve! Hurry up and we can get the lot of them!"

There was a wild scramble in the brush and three men were desperately pumping their bicycles in a mad race to get away down the road. Guns and belts of bullets were strewn over the road in their haste. Brian sent a final shot close above their heads. There was an additional clatter on the blacktop, and they streaked off at an even higher speed.

In the stream, the horses splashed and plunged, but with the end of the gunfire, the farmers managed to lead them up the low bank to the road.

Cermak was at Brian's elbow.

"What was that?"

"Ambush," said Brian. "They were hidden in the brush along the road down there."

"Ah," said Cermak, "kill the farmers and take the horses."

Brian took a careful look around, then walked down toward the farmers.

There were, he saw, four of them. Two were ripping up shirts to bandage a man who was wounded. The other farmer, a burly man of about sixty, smiled broadly and walked over to Brian with outthrust hand.

"Friend, I'll never be happier if I live to be a hundred! That gun of yours was the sweetest music I've ever heard."

Brian gripped his hand. "For the last week we've been shot at from about every farmhouse we've passed. Now I see the reason."

The farmer nodded. "It's gotten so a man can't turn his back without getting a bullet in it. You can't live unless there's enough of you to stand guard day and night." He shook his head. "That's why people shoot at strangers. My

78

name's Ed Barnaby. You and your friends move in with me till you're rested up, and maybe you'll think better of us."

Cermak and the others came down and the wagons made their way along the road. With the addition of the guns and ammunition left behind by the ambushers, they made a formidable party.

Ed Barnaby explained that they'd taken the wagons to get grain left behind at the farm of his friend, Dave Schmidt, who had moved in with him.

"You see," he said as they traveled slowly through the gathering dusk, "we've got plenty of room. It's a big house, and there's just me, my wife, my three boys and two girls; and now my neighbor Dave Schmidt and his family. That sounds like a lot, but when you see the house, you'll see there's plenty of room."

The house was a dazzling white in the moonlight, standing among tall trees that arched above its steep, black-painted metal roof. It stood three full stories high, with tall windows, and a porch that ran around two sides on the ground and second floors. A two-story, L-shaped addition, apparently added as an afterthought, was itself as large as an ordinary house.

"My Granddad wanted lots of room," Ed Barnaby said with a broad, appreciative grin. "He had fourteen children, ten of them boys."

Brian slept that night in a room with delicately flowered, silvery wallpaper, on a soft bed with crisp clean sheets and light warm covers. The next day they had pancakes and sausages for breakfast, and Ed Barnaby showed them the springhouse, dairy barn, chicken coop, smokehouse, hog pen, stable, icehouse, pond, and a small blacksmith shop.

"Grandfather," said Barnaby, "believed in being self-sufficient. I think we can make out all right, so long, that is, as we can keep from being shot dead or burned alive. Grandfather could probably have handled that problem, too, but I'm not so sure Dave Schmidt and me have the right idea. If we'd known what we were doing, we'd never have got caught in that stream bed the way we did. Now, I've watched you boys, and it seems to me you know how to handle yourselves. If you'd care to rest a little before going on west, we'd be glad to board you, if you'd guard the place for us."

Brian and the others liked the idea. While Barnaby and his people worked in the fields, Brian, Carl, Smitty and Steve Cermak made sure no one raided the farm. They studied the layout of the buildings and showed Barnaby the places where it was easiest to get in. Barnaby had two of his sons drive in several lines of fence posts, and Brian and Carl put up barbed wire. They cut down one of the trees, and several bushes that obscured the view from the house. Now, from the cover of the big building, those inside could fire on anyone who tried to tamper with the fences. Then they built a small, sturdy platform around the trap door opening on the roof of the house, and they had a view out over the barn and outbuildings, where one man or woman could serve as a lookout while the others worked.

They'd been there a week when they began to feel well rested and ready to move on.

"I hate to see you go," said Barnaby as they were eating a big dinner. "We've been getting our work done for the first time since this trouble started. We've been getting our sleep, too. I used to jump awake two or three times a night thinking I'd heard somebody out in the barn. I hope you won't leave unless you've got to."

The others eagerly joined in, offering to help stand guard at night, and then a shrill whisle, the prearranged signal for trouble, interrupted the meal.

Carl, who'd been on watch on the roof, came down the stairs fast.

Ed Barnaby said, "What is it? Should we get our guns?"

"Yes, but stay hidden and don't shoot unless the other side shoots first! There are hundreds of them!"

While the others took up their positions inside the house, Brian and Ed Barnaby, each carrying their guns, went out on the porch.

Dozens of armed men, their guns at the ready, stood at the line of fence posts that stretched across the front lawn. The barbed wire lay in lengths on the grass, each strand cut off where it had been stapled to the posts. The men waiting by the fence posts watched the house and buildings alertly. At the center of the lawn stood a man with a whistle raised to his lips, watching the house and waiting.

Back of this line, men trudged past on the road, in a long column, four abreast. The men carried guns, and, watching closely, Brian began to notice significant details.

Every twelve men, there was a break in the column. The men at the head of each file were armed with semi-automatic weapons—often M1 rifles or carbines. The second men carried rifles, usually Springfields or American Enfields. The third men carried shotguns. After that, there was a miscellany of sporting rifles, shotguns, and foreign weapons, until at the end of the line, the third men from the end carried shotguns, the second men from the end carried rifles, often Springfields or Enfields, and the last men carried semi-automatic weapons.

Now, as they marched past, Brian could see that at the head and tail of each section another man walked at the head of the files on the left side of the column.

Barnaby murmured, "Look businesslike, don't they?"

"There's a break every so often when they go by. What's that for?" Brian wondered.

"They're formed in units. Apparently there are four twelve-men squads, the squad leaders marching in front, the assistant squad leaders in the rear. The four squads make up a platoon, with the platoon leaders marching on the far side of the columns."

"What's this coming now?"

Down the road came four men abreast, carrying heavier guns than any they'd seen till now. Behind them came four men carrying light loads of ammunition, and behind them four more men heavily loaded with ammunition.

"Those," said Brian, "are automatic rifles. Whoever's running this has it all organized."

Next came four men pulling a small light cart carrying a water-cooled thirty-caliber machine gun, and four more men pulling another light cart loaded with ammunition. Behind that came a man leading a saddle horse, and beside him a tall, dreamy-looking man wearing on his dark-brown hair a thin band of silver ornamented with slightly raised

81

crests that flashed and glittered in the sunlight. As Brian watched in astonishment, this man raised his right hand; there was a barked command and a single blast on a trumpet. The column came to an abrupt halt. Another shouted command followed, the armed men turned to face the farm buildings, the officers came through the intervals of the line, and the tall man with the band of silver flashing on his head stepped to the horse and swung into the saddle.

For an instant Brian expected the whole line to come forward in a rush, but then the high, clear, carrying voice of the man in the saddle reached out, its tone reasonable, appealing.

"Farmers, just a word before we march on. If the crops are to be planted in good season, they have to be planted now. But no man can work in the fields and stand guard with a gun at the same time. If we're to avoid starvation later, we have to get rid of these killers and arsonists *now!*

"We all know that for weeks you've had to fight off these human rats. You've been held back and slowed down because you had to struggle with the vermin. That's over with. Now you can put away your guns and plow and plant to your heart's content. The Day of the Rat is over." He beamed and swept his hand to indicate the men around him, then he raised his clenched fist. "Right here is the Cat!"

There was an involuntary murmur of approval from the house, and then a roaring cheer from the men in the road.

The farmers were out on the porch, talking excitedly, and the armed men on the road had broken formation and were on the lawn opening boxes of dry rations and taking mugs of steaming coffee and cocoa from men who carried trays from a wagon in the road.

Schmidt, the neighbor who lived with Barney, said excitedly, "Sounds like they mean business."

Barnaby looked at the guns and grinned. "They're equipped to *do* business!" He glanced at Brian. "What do you think?"

The best Brian could manage was to say, "It could be."

Brian was looking at the flashing silver circlet on the tall man's head.

Carl had come out on the porch, to be followed by a dubious-looking Smitty and an expressionless Cermak. Carl glanced around, noting the way the men were spreading out in the shade under the trees, then went back in the house.

Cermak glanced at Brian, and said dryly, "What do you think of that guy, Brian?"

"What he *said* was all right. But what's that crown for?"

Smitty was watching the corner of the house where the porch ran around the other side. "I don't know if you noticed, but one of those people just came up onto the porch with a sheet of paper and a stapler. It looks to me like he tacked up some kind of notice."

Brian saw the man go down the steps. "Let's take a look."

They walked around the corner, to find, stapled to the wall, a large oblong of heavy white paper bearing in small black print a long series of paragraphs. Brian's eye skimmed rapidly over large sections of print as he read the more outstanding points:

NOTICE

Owing to the disastrous failure of electric power throughout this region, be it resolved:

1) That this country, and those districts contiguous to it, shall unite for common defense and be known hereafter as the Districts United.

2) That the inhabitants of these Districts United shall act toward the creation of conditions in which unlawful elements shall be eliminated.

Toward these desirable ends, the following measures are hereby set in motion:

1) Since outside criminal elements are carrying out their practices of killing, arson, robbery, and bushwhacking, a new crime has come into existence, which shall hereinafter be known as "karb," from the initial letters of the criminal acts referred to. Therefore, a Defense Force is hereby created. This Defense Force shall eliminate all criminals practicing karb, by hanging, shooting, decapitation, or whatever other method.

2) To facilitate swift and purposeful action in eliminating karb, a commander of the Defense Force is appointed, who shall be known hereafter as the Districts United Karb Elim-

inator, or, from the initial letters of the words, D.U.K.E., which may be shortened to DUKE or Duke.

3) The duties of the D.U.K.E. shall be to care for and control the Defense Force, restrict and eliminate karb, and endeavor to create those conditions in which work can be carried on without unlawful interruption.

4) Toward this end, the following rules are hereby put into effect . . .

There followed a long list. By order of the D.U.K.E., any foreclosure of mortgages or other sale or exchange of farm properties was suspended. By order of the DUKE, all money taxes on land were revoked. By order of the Duke, all money taxes on income or property were revoked. There then followed a list of taxes payable in storable foods of various kinds, in firewood and in hay, grain, and livestock. To avoid the wrong persons being shot or hanged, and to make things easier for the flying squads of karb-eliminators, no one might travel without a permit from the Duke's local representative. At the end was a paragraph to the effect that any grievance or complaint could be taken to the Duke.

"Nice," said Cermak dryly. "The Duke is everything."

Smitty said, "Look how the notice is signed."

Brian and Cermak studied the imperious scrawl at the bottom of the paper. The signature itself was impossible to decipher but below it were the printed words, "Charles, Duke of the Districts United."

"He's got the thing organized, justified, and explained," Smitty said, "so if you read it sentence by sentence it seems almost reasonable. And, of course, the Duke himself forbids mortgage foreclosures and taxes, and will punish karb and right wrongs. The food taxes are put in sort of anonymously —just some unavoidable thing that had to be done."

"What he's setting up is a feudal system," Brian commented. "The farmers are tied to their land, and pay part of their crops in return for protection. The ruler controls the armed force, makes the laws himself, and administers justice. Same thing as in the Middle Ages."

Cermak shook his head. "They say the government is

still holding out in the northwest—in Montana and Oregon. I think we should head there the first chance we get."

"Yes," said Brian. "And we'd better move fast. It won't be long till they have the lid nailed down tight."

Smitty glanced at several of the Duke's men who were heavily bandaged. "Evidently there are a few people around who don't like being boxed up."

Brian studied them. "It might be worthwhile to know what happened." He moved down the steps, past several of the Duke's men who were joking with the girls of the family, and crossed the lawn to the group of bandaged men. He bumped one of them with his elbow, turned to say "Excuse me," then blinked as if in surprise.

"*You* must have run into trouble."

The man's head was heavily and neatly bandaged, and his left arm was in a sling. But he grinned. "Run into a gang of scientists."

Brian said, "Scientists can't fight, can they?"

One of the other men, his right hand covered by bandages, gave a groan. There were about half a dozen of them, all badly beaten up, and they all glanced at each other. One took a bite out of a loaf of bread sliced lengthwise, a chunk of meat in the middle. Around this mouthful, he said, "I never knowed they could fight, myself. But they learned us a lesson."

Another said, "They hit us with everything. To begin with, they weren't on foot or on horseback. They were driving *trucks*."

Brian looked blank. "Special kind of engine?"

"Diesels. They started them on compressed air. And when old Duke seen them trucks coming toward the cross-roads, he like to run us into the ground getting there first to throw up a roadblock. But that was only the start of the fun. We must have outnumbered them . . . anyway, ten to one, but they had machine guns, hand grenades, and flame-throwers, and just for variety every now and then an arrow would fly out of one of them trucks and somebody'd get skewered. I'd have let them go, myself. We were all getting kind of tired of them. But not old Duke. He was all over us, telling us we *had* to get this bunch, and pretty soon they run low on ammunition, and that flame-thrower of theirs give out, and we got them.

"They had their women and kids with them and everything. Bunch of scientists, headed west. Planned to join up with the Federals up in Montana, near as we could figure. Duke made a deal with them, so now we got the only crew of scientists around here. Duke figures we can use them to make steam cars, fix up locomotives, make gunpowder—lots of things. Only trouble is, they wouldn't strictly promise not to try to get away. Got to be careful they don't sneak out on us."

Brian and the Duke's man were still talking when Carl came up, looking worried, and drew Brian aside.

"Listen," said Carl, "Anne's gone."

"Gone! Where?"

Carl kept his voice low. "We think the Duke's got her."

There was the blast of a whistle, and the Duke's men started back to the road. In a few minutes they were again in formation, and the cooks' helpers were picking up the coffee and cocoa mugs, pieces of waxed paper, and empty ration boxes that were left piled at the base of trees and shrubs. Quickly, Carl explained what had happened.

"Schmidt saw Anne go outside. She wanted to ask her father about something, and said she thought she'd seen him go outside near the fence. She was going to come right back in, but this Duke saw her and called her over. That's the last anyone's seen of her."

Brian looked at the column of troops just starting to move past. Far down the column was a truck, which he recognized as one of Cardan's. He climbed up on the porch, then onto the porch rail, and carefully scanned the marching column.

"There's only one place she could be, Carl. That's in the truck."

Carl bit his lip.

Smitty came over, followed their gaze, and stared at the truck. "That's one of ours!"

Brian jumped down and told him what the Duke's men had said.

"Then," said Smitty, relieved, "they must have gotten away from that crew with the bows and arrows."

"That doesn't help us any if Anne's in that truck."

Cermak had come around the corner of the porch and stopped abruptly. "*Who's* in the truck?"

Brian said, "Carl thinks Anne is gone. We both figure if she's in that column anywhere, it's inside the truck."

Cermak stared at the passing truck. "Yes. He is the Duke. She is the peasant's daughter. If he wants her he will *take* her. Wait a minute while I go inside and make sure."

"Damn it," said Carl, looking at the two guards armed with Tommy guns at the rear of the truck, "how are we going to get her out of there?"

Smitty looked at the platoon coming along behind the truck. They looked particularly well armed and tough.

Slowly the troops moved by.

Cermak, his face carefully blank, came out of the house. "She's gone, all right."

"Whatever we do," said Carl, "we're going to have to do it fast."

Cermak said bitterly, "There isn't a thing we *can* do, and that Duke knows it."

"We *can't* just let her go!" Carl insisted.

"You think she means more to you than she means to me?" Cermak asked. "But I've run my head into too many stone walls not to know another when I see it. Count their guns, then count yours. Go read the notice on the porch. We won't get anywhere against him. But they say the government is still holding out in Montana and a few other states, and sooner or later they're going to have to finish this Duke. Maybe, if I tell them what he's doing, they'll do it now."

Brian said, "I think I see how we could get close enough to keep an eye on her, and maybe get her free later."

Carl said tensely, "How?"

"Join up with them."

Anne's father said angrily, "Don't you think he'll know

enough to suspect your reasons, and put you where you can't do anything?"

Brian again described what he'd learned about the Duke and Cardan.

Carl snapped his fingers. "He wants *scientists!*"

Brian nodded.

Smitty said hesitantly, "*That* might work."

"You do what you want," Cermak said. "I'm going to find what's left of the United States and tell them what's going on here. I know you're doing this for Anne, Brian, but be careful this Duke doesn't suck you in. He'll be clever."

Fifteen minutes later Brian, Carl and Smitty had said good-bye to Cermak and their farmer friends, and were on the road, walking steadily and fast toward the tail of the column on the road ahead.

Before long, they caught up, explained what they wanted, and a tall benevolent figure with glittering ducal coronet greeted them cheerfully, quizzed them briefly on their specialties, and then rubbed his hands together.

"This is a splendid day, gentlemen. I've already captured a number of men scientists, and a woman scientist who was staying at a farm along the way. But you are the first to join me voluntarily." He beamed upon them paternally, then told them where to get shelter halves, blankets, and food when they camped that night. Then he sent for someone to help them get acquainted.

The next day, following stops at several more farms, the Duke and his men set out for their base.

Chapter 10

Built on a low bluff, near the place where a smaller stream joined a river, the Duke's base presented a number of problems to an attacker. It's location made approach tricky from any direction but one, while an impressive tangle of barbed wire blocked the way in that direction. A tall watchtower looked far out over the countryside, making surprise more difficult. The buildings in the camp were completely surrounded by an earth wall and an outer ditch. Like all of the Duke's arrangements that Brian had seen so far, the base had a solid look, as if it were very unlikely to fold up at the first blow.

Brian and his companions had been unable even to catch sight of Anne. They had hoped for better luck at the base, but what they'd seen so far looked unpromising.

Inside, Brian, Carl and Smitty were given quarters in a one-story building about forty feet long. At one end was a small room containing two double bunks. Across the short hall was a lavatory. The rest of the building was empty. Shortly after they'd gotten there, several of the Duke's men carried in a box containing an assortment of books, most of them high-school texts in chemistry, physics and biology, and a plain wooden table.

Smitty said dryly, "Now we're all set."

Brian said, "Well, the main thing is to find Anne, then get in touch with Cardan."

"We'll have a swell time doing it. Did you notice the layout on the way in?"

Brian nodded. There had been half a dozen worn, two-story wooden structures side by side in a straight line, with another two-story building placed well back of one end of the line, and the low, one-story building they were in now, set well back of the other end. These buildings were rectangular, and had apparently all been there long before the Duke. In addition, there was a newer-looking, large, square central mess hall, with another square building and the watchtower in a line back of it. The original rectangular buildings and the mess hall, seen from the air, would form sort of jack-o'-lantern's face, the straight line of six buildings, side by side, forming the mouth, the square mess-hall the nose, and the two separated buildings further back, the eyes. The other square building was at a point midway between and slightly above the eyes, with the watchtower in line further above it. In addition, a number of smaller buildings were scattered around without visible pattern. But what Brian and Smitty were thinking about was the particular way these buildings were split up.

When they'd marched in with the others through the gate, they'd found themselves between two lines of strong fence topped with barbed wire. This led directly through a second gate into a large circular yard with the mess hall in the center, and five additional gates leading to the five separated sections of the base. The row of six side-by-side buildings was split in half by the two lines of fence leading in from the outside. The two other widely separated buildings that sat back from the ends of this line were cut off from it by two more fences. The watchtower and the square building back of the mess hall were separated from the other buildings by double lines of fence topped with barbed wire. Each of these separated sections was connected to the others only by a gate to the yard around the mess hall. When they marched in, half the troops promptly turned right through one gate, while the other half went left through another gate. The line of six two-story buildings were evidently barracks. The Duke and certain of his officers and men went to the square building back of the mess hall. That must be the headquarters building.

Brian, Carl and Smitty had been shown into the small building they were now in. There remained only one place on the Duke's base that might house Cardan and his men. That was four fences away, on the opposite side of the Duke's headquarters and watchtower. Anne, if she was actually on the base, was apparently inside the heavily fenced headquarters building.

As Brian was contemplating these obstacles, there was a knock on the door at the end of the large room. A man came in carrying a covered tray and a wicker basket.

"Eats," he said cheerfully. He set the tray and basket on the table. "Duke says to start studying up on steam engines. You want to earn your pay and water, you're going to have to repair one we're bringing in."

Smitty said promptly, "For that, we'll need tools."

"Sure. You'll get tools." He grinned broadly and went out.

Carl said, "What was that about earning our pay *and water*?"

Brian scowled and raised the lid of the tray. The odor of roast beef, boiled onions and baked potatoes drifted out into the room. In the basket were three fresh rolls, split open, butter melting on them.

"There's plenty of food here," he said, "but no water."

Smitty came back into the room from the direction of the washroom. "There are four sinks, a shower, and a variety of other fittings in there. The only thing in the pipes is air."

They looked at the food a moment, then glanced at each other. Smitty said, "Well, we may die of thirst, but I don't plan to die of starvation." He pulled out a roll.

They were finishing a highly satisfying meal when there was a rumble and a clank outside. Brian opened the door and saw a collection of rusty scrap metal being unloaded from a wagon.

Carl came over. "What's *that*?"

Brian swallowed the last of his roll with a dry mouth.

The men on the wagon dropped off a couple of rods with large fittings at one end, swung the wagon around and went out. The gate clanged shut behind him.

Carl turned around and leaned back into the building. "Hey, Smitty!"

Smitty mopped his plate with his roll. "I'll be out in a minute. Look things over and see what you think."

Brian and Carl walked around the pile of parts, but were no wiser at the end than at the beginning. There were, among other things, a large, heavy cast-iron base, a heavy spoked wheel, rods of different shapes and sizes, a cylindrical piece of metal, a good-sized piston, a little tank, odd lengths of pipe, and assorted loose bolts and cap screws. To one side lay a greasy cloth with a hammer and a variety of wrenches and other tools wrapped up in it.

Smitty came out the door of the building wearing a look of contentment, and walked around the pile. He bent over, pulled out one of the rods and examined the large end carefully, got up, and leaned over to pull out another part.

On the far side of the fence, a good dozen of the Duke's

men lounged around, grinning and watching the obvious discomfiture of Brian and Carl.

Smitty straightened up. "It's all here. In fact, some joker has thrown in some extra pieces to foul us up."

"Great," said Carl. "What is it?"

Smitty looked surprised. "It's a low horsepower, side-crank, slide-valve steam engine. See, here's the crosshead, this is the connecting rod, and there's the crankshaft. The whole thing has already been put together and then disassembled. You see the grease here, and the way this rust has been scraped away so the metal is shiny where the parts have been fitted together?"

Carl shook his head. "I'm just manual labor on this job."

Brian was struggling to remember what little he'd ever learned about steam engines.

Smitty said, "Do just as I say. First, bring that table out so we can get some of these parts up out of the dirt. Then we'd better start putting it together. I'm thirsty already."

Under Smitty's directions, they began assembling the engine. At dusk, one of the Duke's men carried out a gasoline lantern which cast its white glare and hard shadows on the scene. Around midnight, the three men, covered with perspiration and dizzy with thirst, stood back from the finished job. They were through.

The piston was connected to the piston rod, the piston rod to the crosshead, the crosshead to the connecting rod, the connecting rod to the crankshaft. The valve gear was all connected up. If they had a source of steam, the thing should work.

There was a clang as the gate opened and three men came in carrying buckets of water, while a fourth man looked over the engine, grinned, and said, "Okay, you'll do. The Duke'll see you tomorrow morning at eight." He nodded to the others, who set down the water.

Brian, Carl and Smitty drank the cool water cautiously, like men who have crossed the desert and are afraid to take too much at once. They fell into their bunks, exhausted —only to be blasted out of bed by a bugle thrust in the nearest doorway. They were sure they'd slept about an hour;

it turned out to be six a.m. The roar of a megaphone invited them out for half an hour of violent calisthenics. A tray containing three steaming bowls of corn-meal mush was delivered to them at seven ten, followed by another six buckets of water. A small wood stove was lugged into the room, and several men were connecting it up as Brian, Carl and Smitty trudged sleepily out to the gate and said, "We're supposed to see the Duke at eight. Where do we find him?"

"At the palace. Through that gate to the left."

The "palace" turned out to be the large square headquarters building near the watchtower. This had a porch completely around the base and the second floor, with several business places, namely the Palace Barber Shop, the Palace Refreshment Stand, and the Palace Clothes and Equipment Mart, on the first floor. Beside a broad flight of stairs to the second floor was a sign in the shape of an arrow, with the letters D.U.K.E.

The second-floor porch, running completely around the building, had a variety of doors opening off it. To Brian's right as he left the steps was a door marked D.U.K.E. Against the wall nearby was a large grandfather clock, plainly put there as a hint to people to come and leave on time. The clock now said three minutes before eight. On the other side of the door from the clock stood a guard, who watched them with no particular expression.

"We're early," Brian commented. "If we go in now, he'll be mad. Let's walk around for a few minutes."

Smitty grunted. "Good idea."

The guard paid no special attention as they took the lucky opportunity to walk around to the opposite side of the building, where the porch looked down over the two-story building that they thought must house Cardan and his men. As they watched, a broad, powerfully built man with a frayed cigar stub clenched in the corner of his mouth opened the door at the end of the building, and nodded to someone within.

Unnecessarily, Carl murmured, "That's Cardan."

From within, a tall blond man, and a sharp-featured man with dark hair, stepped out carrying a box containing dull whitish oblongs about four inches long by three wide.

Smitty said in a low voice, "Soap."

Brian caught his breath.

Just then, there was the sound of a door closing around the corner of the building, and the Duke's voice was low but clear.

"My dear," said the Duke, "I could end your resistance very easily. But I want your decision to be freely made."

Anne's voice carried a trace of exasperation. "I've already told you my decision."

"But that's the *wrong* decision. You don't know what you're trying to throw away. I offer you position which no one else in this world can offer. Don't smile. Already I control this base and the outlying camps. I have brought peace and order to a region that would have been lost to starvation and murder. This is only the beginning. Through the entire country, there's a crying need for peace, order and central direction. There is a need, and I supply the lack. What you see now is just the beginning of a snowball."

The voices were coming closer.

Brian and his companions went quietly down the porch in the opposite direction, and were waiting outside the Duke's office when, looking exasperated but stubborn, he walked in and was immediately all cordiality as he invited them inside and congratulated them on putting the steam engine together. He pulled aside a curtain on the wall to reveal a map of the roads and railroads of the state. The eastern part of the map was thickly crisscrossed with lines indicating tracks.

"As of now," said the Duke, "there are three means of rapid transportation here: horse, bicycle, and diesel truck started by compressed air. The horse has a top speed of, say, thirty-five miles an hour, and can't sustain it for more than a few minutes. The bicycle can go fifty miles an hour downhill, and up the same hill it goes one mile an hour with the rider pushing. Neither can carry much of anything as baggage, and in a storm the rider is fully exposed to the weather. The diesel truck can go fifty or sixty miles an hour over a long distance, carrying a considerable load, but we have a certain amount of difficulty supplying suitable fuel, and this will get worse before it gets better.

THE DAY THE MACHINES STOPPED

"In addition, the same thing that now blocks electricity seems to weaken the metal itself, and this engine relies for power on a rapid series of violent explosions inside the cylinders. As a result, the engines have to be pulled apart every few days. In short, we have nothing but unreliable means of rapid transportation at our disposal. This limits the radius of effective control of any military force we can form. It means that the only practical defense against anarchy is the creation of many small independent units, each self-sufficient and capable of defense against roving gangs of arsonists and murderers."

The Duke's fist banged on the desk. His eyes flashed. As Brian and the others waited alertly for an explosion of temper, the Duke beamed upon them.

"It won't do. I visualize in its place a mighty organization of steam locomotives, each capable of fueling by coal or wood, knitting together a network of armed camps under my own control, devoted to keeping order, eliminating karb, and bringing in supplies and recruits throughout a continuously expanding region. Such locomotives, pulling short trains, could average between forty and forty-five miles an hour, and travel, if need be, a thousand miles a day. They could do it without excessive strain or wear on the metal, and they could easily carry loads that would be too heavy for transportation by road. They would enable me to switch troops from one place to another very rapidly, and to unite a large region under one centralized control." He leaned back and beamed upon them. "The people who did the work that put this tool at my disposal would be very liberally rewarded."

Brian and the others went back to their little building with a clear picture of what the Duke had in mind.

"That So-and-So," said Smitty, "sees himself as a dictator, with a fleet of locomotives carrying his private army around the country from one place to another."

"Sure," said Carl. "And he can do it, too. People will be so glad to get the gangs off their necks that they won't realize they've been taken over till it's too late."

Brian said, "Anne's father was right. We've got to find

out if there's some piece of America left somewhere, and join up with it."

"Remember, he's got Anne," Carl reminded.

"We know where she is, anyway—and where Cardan is," said Smitty.

Brian glanced out the window at the double fence, "We've got to find some way to get in touch with them."

Outside their door, there was the crash of metal.

Smitty swore.

The door opened. One of the Duke's men said, "This came out of an old lumber mill. Duke wants it working again. You get your water when she works. Let us know if you need anything."

Outside was a formidable heap of scrap that made what they'd worked on the night before look brand-new.

In the next few weeks, Brian, Carl and Smitty repaired eight old steam engines. Food, fuel, clothing, special privileges—and water—were their rewards. The first thing any of them knew of a new job was the sound of its being unloaded and the announcement that they would get water when they had it finished. They took to hoarding water in the sinks and washtubs, but there was a limit to the amount they could store, while there was no limit to the rusted, stuck, cracked, corroded antique engines they were supposed to repair.

At night, when they were between jobs, Brian, Smitty and Carl tested the fences around their part of camp, and discovered an ingenious system of spring-loaded bells that immediately announced any attempt to get over the top. They could not cut the fence itself without it being discovered the next day, and the bottom of the fence turned out to be set in concrete. After a great deal of nighttime exploration, they finally found a weak place under the fence leading to a space between the outer wall and the fence surrounding the Duke's "palace." At the other end of this narrow passage was the place where Brian had seen Cardan, Maclane and Donovan; and here, too, was a spot where the fence could be burrowed under. While Smitty stayed behind in case a guard should come on one of the infrequent checks, Brian and Carl succeeded one cloudy night in getting under both fences, making their way through the darkness to Cardan's building, easing open the door, and getting in, only to be immediately knocked senseless for their pains.

Brian opened his eyes in a room lighted brightly by a kerosene lamp, with blankets over the windows, and the harsh flat planes of a man's face regarding him through a cloud of cigar smoke.

Brian recognized Cardan and, behind him, the sharp features of Maclane.

Brian dizzily sat up. His voice came out in a croak. "Hello, Chief."

Cardan answered with a bare grunt and glanced at Carl, who was looking around dazedly.

Brian sniffed, aware, through the smell of cigar smoke, of a complex of faint odors that might conceivably come from glycerine and a mixture of nitric and sulfuric acids at work.

He risked a guess. "I hope you're keeping it cool."

Cardan looked at him, then glanced at Donovan. "How's this batch coming?"

"Slow, as usual. We don't want any accidental reactions."

"When are you planning to get out?" Brian asked.

Cardan looked thoughtfully at the glowing tip of his cigar and considered the question. "Possibly next week. Do *you* have any plans?"

"First we wanted to get in touch with you. We're too worn out pounding on antique steam engines to plan very far ahead."

"That explains why the pressure on us let up a little," Cardan said.

Brian asked, "What can we do to help?"

"There isn't much you can do," said Cardan, "except to keep caught up on your work and do nothing to make them suspicious. As for how we're going to get out, you may have noticed a big piece of wheeled machinery on your way in."

Brian shook his head. "It's black as pitch out there."

"Well," said Cardan, "there's an antique steam tractor out there. This so-called Duke wants it rebuilt and fitted with a blade—to make a kind of steam-powered bulldozer. We plan to distract attention with several dynamite blasts on the far side of camp, use the bulldozer to shove the wall into the ditch, and get away in the steam cars and diesel trucks that are in for repairs at the time. We can't tell just what night will be right, but we'll let you know when it comes."

"What about Anne?"

Cardan took the cigar out of his mouth. "Is she here?"

Brian told what had happened, and Cardan thought a moment. "We could rig up something to immobilize the stretched wires that work that alarm system, then we could cut the fence, put a ladder up the side of that building and get her out that way. First, we'll have to find out what room she's in, but I'm sure we can do that."

Brian didn't like the idea of standing aside while the others did the work, but Cardan insisted.

"This has been planned for a long time, and we can't change it now. Don't worry. Just keep on as you have been. Don't do anything to arouse suspicion. We want to keep them happy till we blast our way out of this place. Just go on as you are till our man crawls in and tells you to clear out."

Doing as Cardan said and sticking to their usual routine was maddening, and to avoid thinking of the escape, they worked harder than ever. The Duke was delighted with them.

Soon they were at work in a large machinery shed, newly built between the palace and the watchtower. Here everything seemed to go wrong. Boilers were clogged, mechanical power-transmission lines tore themselves loose, engines vibrated, safety valves stuck, then let go with a roar and refused to close, governors ran the engines fast, then slow, then fast again, in a maddening rhythm that drove them to distraction; and in the midst of this chaos, the Duke came in covered with soot and dragged them outside for a look at their half-collapsed smokepipe. Only gradually did they begin to straighten out the chaos. And then one night Brian woke to hear Carl say urgently, "Come on, Brian! The chief says we're leaving!"

Brian stumbled to his feet, dressed rapidly, and stepped to the door. As he went out, there was a dull impact at the back of his head, a burst of dazzling lights, and he felt himself falling.

His last conscious thought as he spiraled into blackness was the realization that Carl had done it again . . .

Somewhere, there was a heavy explosion, shouts, and the sounds of running feet. Then there was another explosion, the sound of shouts, a raining of dirt, pebbles, the thud of falling rocks, shouted orders, and a blast that seemed to go on forever.

A glare of light appeared, and a rough voice said, "There's one, Duke! There's one that didn't get away!"

Rough hands gripped Brian by the arms.

An open hand slapped him stingingly across the face.

The light glared in his eyes, and the Duke was looking at him with a cold intensity.

Chapter 11

Brian, seeing the spot he was in, groped for some way out. Before the Duke had the chance to speak, Brian said angrily, "Did that yellow-haired Judas get away?"

The Duke looked puzzled, then turned as two of his men came over, supporting a battered and swearing Smitty.

A look of perfect mutual understanding passed between Brian and Smitty. If Smitty had had any lingering doubt as to what had caused Brian's original delay in joining the rest of Cardan's men, it was gone now. Angrily, he said to Brian, "I tried to catch him, but he got away."

Brian said, "He smashed me over the head and knocked me senseless."

"I know. Then I chased him, and he cracked *me* over the head. He jumped into some kind of truck and a whole bunch of people went right out through the wall."

Smitty was obviously trying the same gambit that had occurred to Brian. The only trouble was that, first, it all rang slightly false to Brian's ears; and second, if the Duke separated them, they would have no chance to get together on a story. Brian might say one thing and Smitty something else. The only chance they had seemed to come from the unmistakable indignation in their voices. The men around the Duke looked puzzled. The Duke himself glanced first at Brian, then at Smitty, as if urging them to go on.

But Brian, who'd had very little practice in misrepresenting things, was afraid of the fantastic and transparent web of lies he might spin if he once got started. Smitty, on the other hand, had no way to know what Brian might already have said, and was afraid to go on for fear he might contradict him.

The Duke was glancing impatiently from one to the other when Brian realized Smitty's predicament.

With silence now stretched to the breaking point, there rose from the depths of Brian's subconscious a liar's credo that he had heard somewhere: *Always stick as close to the truth as possible—only change what has to be changed.*

With this for a guide, Brian said, "Something woke me up. I said, 'Carl?' Then he said something like 'The chief wants us outside.' So I got dressed and came out. The instant I opened the door there was a blinding flash, and the next thing I remember there were rocks and dirt raining down around me."

The Duke remained silent, but one of the Duke's men said, "How come you knew it was Carl? It was dark in the room, wasn't it?"

Brian perspired. He had uttered only four sentences and already he was trapped.

Smitty got him out of it. "Carl would get up and prowl around at night." This was true enough, as, before Cardan's warning, all three of them had prowled around at night.

THE DAY THE MACHINES STOPPED

The Duke glanced at Brian. "Carl said, 'The chief wants us outside.' And you thought he meant me?"

Brian realized that this had been another mistake, but he managed a convincing shrug. "Who else?"

One of the Duke's men said, "That's what the rest of the scientists called the head scientist who smokes the cigars—chief."

"Then," said the Duke, "evidently Carl found some way to get to the others, and threw in with them. Just as he was leaving, someone called him, and he was nervous and afraid he'd be followed, so—" The Duke glanced at Brian. "Let's feel that bump." Brian winced as the Duke's fingers probed the tender spot, and then the Duke said, "Obviously, these two were fighting on our side. Let them go so they can check the machine shed for us."

Brian and Smitty were greatly relieved by the Duke's leniency with them, but not by the change that came over the base as the Duke pointed out to his shame-faced followers what could have happened if this had been an attack instead of an escape. Discipline was tightened up, and Brian and Smitty found themselves constantly guarded—not, apparently, because the Duke really distrusted them, but just to be on the safe side. In the next few weeks the new and stricter routine became solidly established, and Brian and Smitty couldn't see the slightest possibility for escape.

The Duke's most distant patrols reported the successful escape of Cardan's men, Anne, and Carl. Anne, the Duke never mentioned, but he determinedly put his energies into repairing the damage done to his base and his plans.

By now, the Duke had acquired more old steam engines and steam cars. Some he wanted made very light and fast. Some he wanted made into the equivalent of armored tanks. Others were to be shielded around the engine and part of the cargo section, and equipped to carry heavy loads of water and fuel. Gradually, a steam-powered armored force came into existence, capable of moving over the roads in a body at thirty or forty miles an hour by day.

The steam-powered workshop in the shed was now equipped with power lathes, drills, saws, and a blacksmith

101

shop. The Duke was selecting the best-fitted of his men to do skilled work, and the competition was keen because of the relief from the continuous exercises and drills.

By now, the Duke's men had regular ranks and insignia, and a standard uniform to be worn at all times except when off duty. But the men were busy and off-duty hours were rare. Flying squads of cavalry roamed the countryside hunting for "karbists." The Duke's armored force prowled the roads and highways, spotting towns that had been taken over by gangs, sending word back to the base by fast steam-car, and often by their mere appearance overawing and demoralizing the gangs before the infantry arrived in short trains of steam-drawn wagons.

Brian went along on one of these trips, huddled between the driver and the gunner, sucking in oven-hot air and feeling his nerve-ends tingle at the thought of what could happen if a high-velocity bullet should slam through the improvised armor and pierce the boiler. His experiences led him to provide heavier armor for selected parts of the steam cars, relocate the boilers, and put in a device to provide ventilation for the men.

He and Smitty now had in mind what they could do if they could only get one of the faster steam cars fueled and ready, and a half-hour's head start. But now the Duke's guards were perpetually alert, kept that way by special exercises, by a squad of daredevil "guard-catchers" whose job it was to get past careless guards, and by a merit system that brought extra privileges to guards who halted the "guard-catchers" with a shouted warning, and extra kitchen-duty to those who failed to spot them in time.

The Duke's men were gradually becoming an elite corps, with the pride of such an organization, and while they regarded Brian as one of themselves, he could not get out because he lacked the proper pass, and the Duke saw to it that either he or Smitty was always on strenuous duty at the base when the other was out.

Late spring turned to summer. The Duke's territory expanded, and his army grew with the volunteer sons of farmers and town dwellers, eager for the chance to rid the country of outlaws and parasites.

As the summer passed, the Duke's control reached farther, and became stronger at the same time. Brian and Smitty were kept working on steam locomotives, and they now had a trained crew to help them. By fall, the crew was doing all the maintenance work, and Brian and Smitty had a combined laboratory and office in a workshop that had grown to the size of a small factory.

One day in late fall, Brian looked up from a new chemical bench, and realized that he was no nearer to Montana than he had been that spring. He was here. Anne—and Carl—were there. And the chances of escape were worsening. It was no longer possible to escape the Duke's grasp by going thirty miles away. His control now stretched out for well over a hundred miles, with the fast steam-cars providing a delivery and messenger service that knit the whole together. Brian himself had helped work out the compound for the signal flares and design the mirrors that soon would be used to flash warnings and messages from one end of the Duke's domain to the other, along a special chain of stations centering at his headquarters. At a word of command, the roads could be blocked and the guard posts alerted for fugitives. If Brian was going to escape, he should do it now.

But Brian was determined to escape with Smitty, and the Duke chose this time to send Smitty out with a crew to repair a steam locomotive that had just been found by a scouting party.

Time passed.

The chain of signal stations was completed, the guards remained as alert as ever, and then the countryside was deep in snow, the streams iced over, and the mercury hovering around zero.

One evening in the pit of winter, when the temperature had plunged deeper yet, the Duke sent for Brian. After questioning Brian closely on the progress of his work, the Duke leaned back in his big chair and put his feet on the shiny bumper of a cast-iron stove that radiated a steady comforting warmth.

"You've done well, Brian," said the Duke expansively. "You don't mind if I call you Brian, do you?"

"No, of course not," said Brian, puzzled by the sudden friendliness.

"I've watched you," said the Duke, beaming, and pulling over a kind of humidor on wheels. "You've done good work."

"Thank you, sir."

"Even though," said the Duke, opening the lid of the container and taking out some cheese crackers, "you've wasted a certain amount of time trying to find some chance to get away."

Brian started to protest.

The Duke paused with the crackers and smiled. "People become leaders, not because they understand test tubes or bank balances, but because they understand *people*."

Brian looked at him a moment, then said, "How long have you known this?"

"Since the night the others got away. I'd suspected it before that time. Of course, I knew Cardan and the others wanted to get away. What I didn't appreciate was their ingenuity. You see, I lacked the technical knowledge to realize what they could do. It was the soap, wasn't it?"

"The soap?"

"A by-product of soap manufacture," said the Duke, "is glycerin." He waved to a small shelf of books nearby. "I've been more careful since that experience. They made soap for us, and glycerin for themselves. From the glycerin, by the proper procedure, nitroglycerin can be prepared. And from nitroglycerin can be made dynamite. Just what the exact steps they followed were, I don't know." He was watching Brian alertly, with an expression of good humor. "I'm suprised to see that you're interested rather than uneasy. Apparently, *you* didn't make it for them, after all."

Brian shook his head. "I suspected the whole thing when I saw the soap carried out—that is, I suspected they were making explosive, and could use it to get away—but I was too busy working on steam engines to have helped them, even if I'd wanted to."

"Nevertheless, you'd planned to leave with them." It wasn't a question but a statement.

"Anything I might say," said Brian, forcing a smile,

"would tend to incriminate me. But if you knew this then, why did you accept our story?"

"Why not? I needed you. And it was obvious that you'd missed the opportunity to get away. The only question was, would the men believe you? If not, I would have to devise a punishment that would satisfy their anger, while still enabling you to recover and be of use. I've never seen a worse liar, but with my help, luckily you convinced the men that you were innocent."

Brian speechlessly accepted the dish of crackers the Duke held out to him.

The Duke peered into his box on wheels, extracted two mugs and a large Thermos bottle, and filled the mugs with steaming cocoa. "There's nothing like a fire and a cup of good hot cocoa when it's twenty below outside. Yes, the situation was very bad that night, and the best I could make of it didn't correct it entirely."

"Certainly discipline was tightened up. You've gained a lot of territory since then."

"True, but against the petty opponents I've had to contend with, territory is easy to gain. It can be lost just as quickly to superior opponents. It's necessary to look ahead and consider the caliber of the opposition. In that light, the loss of Cardan and his men was very possibly fatal. Our organization here is primitive, and we need everything we can get in the form of scientific and engineering skill to strengthen us against the opposition."

Brian was puzzled. "What *is* the opposition?"

"The old habits and patterns of thought from before the disaster. New organizations, I can deal with. But to the northwest, the old pattern still holds. I thought for a time that it would die out, be extinguished in the disorder. But it has survived, and now it extends itself with lightning rapidity. When the old trumpet sounds with all its power, then the people rally to the old flag, and the banners of the new look cheap and shoddy. People obey me now because they judge me against a background of ruin and chaos. Let them see me for a time in comparison with things as they were before the disaster, and I will appear little. Let there be a choice between me and the old flag, and I will be lucky if my own men stick with me. *That* is why the loss of Cardan was a possible deathblow. He went to the northwest, and when he went, that block of scientific and engineering skill was transferred from me to them."

The Duke paused, the cocoa cup half raised, and his eyes gazing off as if he looked into a different world that Brian couldn't see.

"Before the escape of Cardan, the Federals were going under. Only one state and parts of two others still flew the old flag and held to the old ways. And the chaos was spreading, threatening to submerge them even there. Then it was as if the old way, in its death struggle, sent out a call for whoever was still faithful. Cardan heard that call, and he went. He wasn't the only one. For weeks around that time there was a flow of men, young and old, leaving here for the northwest. We stopped some, but we couldn't stop all. And it wasn't only hands and guns that went north. Brains went north, too. A few months later their crisis was broken. And that is the opposition I'll be measured against someday."

Brian listened in astonished silence, noting a strange shine in the Duke's eyes as he spoke of the old flag.

"Why," said Brian, "if you feel that way—?"

The Duke raised his hand. "I came into the world from a direction that gave me a poor perspective on the old ways. Let's not talk of that. Let's talk of what we have here. Everyone in my organization is looked after. There is no graft, no crookedness. Karbists are destroyed on sight, not left to burden and poison the rest. Child-killers and dope-runners lead a short life here. Every man is honest, because he knows that in his honesty he has the full power of the organization behind him. You've seen order brought out of chaos, and the countryside made safe for honest men who are willing to work."

The Duke talked on, and what he said seemed true. Brian felt his personal power, and, somewhere in the background of his mind, he was always aware that the man could snap his fingers, say, "Kill this man," and Brian would be killed.

"What I've done," the Duke went on, "I've been able to

do because I understand people. But I need someone who understands *things*. I need a right-hand man who can run the mines and factories, who can knit the broken bits into a smooth-running system. I need someone like that, and so does the whole country. I offer you this job, and with it, authority and power second only to my own."

For an instant, Brian wavered. Then abruptly he saw the fallacy in the Duke's position. As in other dictatorships, the power was concentrated in one man. But even if one man survived the power without delusions of grandeur, what happened if he was shot, died of heart failure, or fell down a staircase? Immediately, everything would be thrown into chaos. In this case, Brian would be second in command, but he would have been put there by the Duke, and his power would rest on the Duke, who would be gone. Inevitably, there would be a power struggle. Granted that the Duke had shown skill and restraint in the use of his power, what assurance was there that the next man would do the same?

The Duke, seeing Brian's hesitation, smiled. "I can understand your hesitation. But I wouldn't offer you this if I weren't sure that you could do the job, and that you wouldn't misuse the power. But there's no need to decide right now. Think it over."

That discussion was the first of many that Brian had as the subzero cold held military operations to a standstill, and the Duke craved companionship and conversation in the long winter evenings. One night, he raised the question of the disaster that had caused the trouble.

"A clever device," said the Duke. "It has us hamstrung, tied in knots. I wonder how fast the Russians are progressing while we are still trying to get back on our feet?"

Brian, convinced that the Russians had been hurt as much as anyone, argued that the disaster had resulted from an accident. The Duke nodded. "Maybe. But it so nearly collapsed our whole structure that it's hard to think it could have been *entirely* accidental."

"I don't know," said Brian. "We'd gotten so that any delay anywhere tended to paralyze the system. A short circuit could knock out power in a whole district. A shipping strike could stop whole industries. Everything was so knit together and interdependent that a failure in any part reacted on the whole."

Another night, toward spring, Brian excused himself on the grounds that he was worn out. The Duke smiled. "You're doing the work. You should have the rank and reward." The next night, the Duke sent for Smitty, who came back close to midnight and said, "I wish I was back with Cardan. This bird is out of his mind. He asked me how I'd like to be a marquis and have everybody bang his head on the floor for me. I think that's what he was talking about. How is a man supposed to do his work when he has to be up half the night talking nonsense?"

It occurred to Brian that the Duke was sending a gentle hint that he was growing impatient. Brian would have to decide soon, one way or the other. This little push decided Brian. He sat up and swung his feet over the edge of the bed. Smitty was by the stove, warming his hands after the icy trip back from the Duke's palace. The room was barely warm, but the floorboards were icy under Brian's bare feet.

"Listen," he said, "are those guards outside again tonight?"

"They're huddled in the anteroom, feeding chunks to the fire. Nobody's *outside*. Out there, you can feel your nostrils congeal and your nose turn blue every time you take a breath."

"I wonder about the guards at the gate."

"They're there, no doubt, and just as cold as everyone else." Smitty turned to thaw himself on another side. "What are you thinking?"

"I noticed on the work sheets that a fast steam car got repaired today. It's ready to go out tomorrow."

Smitty was silent an instant, then he gave a low whistle.

"Ye gods, Brian! Tonight is no night for that. No one in his right mind would go out tonight!"

"That's the point."

"You mean, they wouldn't be expecting it?"

"Of course they wouldn't. You just said so yourself."

Smitty looked out the window, where the icicles dangled five feet long. "I wish I'd kept my mouth shut."

Brian got up and looked out.

A full moon shone on the snow-covered roof and icy ground. Everywhere he could see, the windows were dark and the walks and roadways empty.

Excitedly, he said, "This is our chance. We've been working all this time for the Duke because we had no *chance* to get away. Now is the chance!"

"Brian, *listen—*"

Brian was already taking the blankets from the bed.

Smitty said anxiously, "What are you going to do with them?"

"We're going to rip one into strips and knot them to make a rope. When I'm down there, you throw the other blankets down to me, because we're going to need them in the steam car. But first I'm going to see if I can't write the Duke's signature."

The next forty minutes saw them make their way, fingers stiff with cold, down the improvised rope to the ground, then slip and teeter over the uneven ice to the entrance door of the repair garage.

From the guardroom inside, a voice said, "Come on, Ed, throw in another piece. What ails you?"

"Hit this chunk a crack with your rifle butt, will you? It's froze to the ground."

Smitty, shivering, murmured, "We can break a window in back."

"No," whispered Brian. "They'd hear when we opened the big door."

He knocked on the door. "Open up! Duke's orders!"

The door came open and two rough figures looked out. "My God! What could bring anyone out on a night like this?"

"Fire in the oil field," said Brian. "It came in on the flasher an hour ago. Duke wants it out, and no one there knows how." Brian spread his hands at the stove. "We can blast it out, I hope. First we've got to figure out some way to get near the thing."

"What's the trouble?"

Brian grimaced. "Too hot."

This brought a round of laughter, and if there had been any trace of suspicion, it was gone now.

The guards helped them check the steam car. Oil, water, and gas gauges showed full, the chains were on the wheels, and the fabric top and side-curtains were as tight as they could be made. When steam pressure was built up, the guards folded back the buildings' heavy doors, Brian advanced the speed lever, and the car rolled out smoothly, skidded, crabbed along sidewise on the ice, then straightened out again.

At the gate, Brian thrust out an oblong of paper bearing the date and the printed words, *Give these men every possible assistance*, with a fair imitation of the Duke's scrawl beneath it.

The men in the gatehouse turned up the oil lamp and, in the glow from the smoked-up lamp chimney, huddled over the little piece of paper, then asked, "What's broke loose that he sends you out on a night like this?"

Brian told the same story he'd told the other guards. It brought the same laugh, then the paper was handed back.

Brian eased the car forward as a powerful crank raised the gate, to the sound of a heavy snap as the base of the gate broke loose from the ice. Then they were outside.

Already, as they pulled their blankets around them, they could feel their feet growing numb.

But behind them, the Duke's base was fading into a dim shadow in the moonlight.

And ahead of them, the frozen road was wide-open, stretching out unguarded into the far distance.

It was daylight when they reached the first of the rare fuel and water stations that dotted the roads at long intervals. To Brian's astonishment, the place was a smoking shambles.

"Chimney caught fire," said one of the men who turned as Brian came over. "The damned fool didn't have the sense to clean the soot out." He looked at Brian's car. "What brings you out in this weather? You after those escapees?"

Brian kept his face straight, nodding. "No chance you'd have noticed them?"

110

"An army could have gone past and we wouldn't have seen it. We had our hands full with this thing."

"When did you get the word?"

"Came over the flasher two hours ago. I wouldn't break my neck if I were you. With the stations closed to all traffic, they'll run out of steam soon enough, or get nailed when they come in for fuel."

Brian went back to the car and told Smitty the bad news. Then they drove in silence till Smitty said, "Look, this country is familiar. This is where we were earlier, before the Duke showed up."

Brian looked around in surprise. "I think you're right."

Twenty minutes later they were in the yard of the Barnaby farm.

"Yes," said the elder Barnaby, "you don't have to say a thing. We know all about it. They had messengers going from house to house on horseback not an hour ago. Now you take the four horses we're raising for the Duke's service, my eldest boy and Ed Schmidt's son, and knock me over the head before you go so I can tell the Cols you took the horses by force and the two boys for hostages."

" 'Cols' ?" said Brian.

"Citizen's Obedience League. I don't know if the Duke planned that or it just grew up naturally, like toadstools where the ground is rotten. If you make it to America, tell them to come as soon as they can. The teaching in the schools here is changed; all the children swear allegiance to the Duke, and the secret police plant spies in every town and every house. My own daughter is in it, and she'd turn me in as soon as she'd spit, except that this mornnig she's away at a group meeting."

Brian stared at him. "That bad? But what do you mean, 'If you make it to America'? This *is* America."

Barnaby shook his head. "No, it isn't. I mean, where they still fly the flag. Where they still *vote*. Tell them the Duke's neat system. First, he ends karb. Everybody's happy, and everybody goes along with his rules. But his rules never end. By the time the karb is wiped out, his representatives have moved in, and everything is split up into compartments. Nobody can move off his place without permission. If you do, you're hanged for a karbist. All it takes is a piece of paper, and your property is redistributed—Duke's orders."

"But you can complain to the Duke!"

"When first you have to go to the local representative for a travel permit?"

Brian shook his head. He looked around and saw two strong boys leading horses that were saddled and ready.

"Smitty," said Brian, "would you see if there are guns in the back of that car? The work sheet said it was a patrol, not a courier car."

Smitty climbed inside and came out carrying two rifles by the slings. Brian saw that they were Springfields. The Duke's choice of weapons coincided with that of Cardan, especially in cold weather, when a complicated action might make trouble. Smitty handed one gun to Brian and one to one of the boys. A moment later he was out with two more rifles, and with bandoliers of ammunition.

"We may have to fight," Brian said. "You can say I told the boys that once I got them out of here they could never turn back. They'd be hanged for violating the no-travel law. That will explain why they fight, if we have to fight."

Barnaby agreed.

The woman came out with water and sandwiches, and put small bags in the pockets of the men's coats. Then Barnaby said, "Now, don't waste any more time. And leave a bump I can use for proof, and a bruise to show where I hit the ground."

Ed Schmidt finally stepped forward. There was a quiet thud, and Barnaby crumpled to the ground.

"On your way," said Schmidt. He glanced at his son. "And mind you, boy, when you shoot, don't waste bullets firing over their heads! Aim for the chest, and leave it to Providence to save the vermin if it's God's Will."

The boy nodded, tears streaming down his cheeks.

The women reached up to kiss their sons good-by, and Schmidt said, "Hurry. We've got to report this."

112

And then Brian and the others were on their way.

The sun was up now, and with it as they rode came a day as unbelievably hot as the night had been cold. To their astonishment, the pleasant warmth of early morning turned into summerlike heat by noon. The glare of the sun on the snow all but blinded them, and ground, heaved up be frost, gave way under the horses' hoofs. Their progress was maddeningly slow.

That night, it was warm, and they could hear the rushing of streams filling up with the run-off from the melted snow. They fed the horses at roofed-over sheds where hay was piled to feed cattle. They slept in the hay, and for food, they added water to some of the mixture of ground dried corn and sugar that the women had put in their pockets. The next day dawned sunny and hot, and that night the two boys "karbed it" at a farmer's smokehouse, returning with enough meat to keep them contented for a few days of travel. Then days and nights blurred together until all they knew was that they were headed north and west, and finally they were out of the Duke's territory. No identifiable sign told them that, but there seemed to be something in the air—a feeling of freedom that Brian had forgotten existed.

It was a little later that they crossed the brow of a hill, and Smitty said, "Look back there."

Brian turned around.

Behind them, far back, were a dozen little dots, spread out over the country in two staggered files, and coming toward them fast.

The Duke's men had found the trail.

Chapter 12

After studying the distance between themselves and their pursuers, and the speed at which the pursuers came, young Barnaby made a suggestion. Instead of a desperate attempt to gain distance, they went at a pace that would spare the horses, moving fast and easily as the Duke's men drove their mounts to ever greater exertions and steadily whittled down the distance. The country was more broken now, and here and there were rocky stretches where a trail was hard to follow. At one of these places, the Duke's men thundered off in the wrong direction, and when they discovered their mistake and turned back, their winded horses began to give out. By nightfall, Brian and the others had more than their lead. The next day, they saw only occasional distant signs of pursuit, and that night, they were confident.

The next morning, the Duke's men were right behind them, and there was nothing to do but make a run for it. But the Duke's men had faster horses. Ahead of them, as they plunged down a hillside, Brian could see a pair of shining railroad tracks, and, off in the distance, a peculiar towerlike structure. Something moved at its peak, and swung back again. What it was, he didn't know and then there was no time to think of it.

Now they were part way up the side of the mountain, and a tumble of rocks offered some refuge so they sprang off to crouch behind the rocks and the four Springfields brought two of their pursuers from the saddles. The others split and raced right and left, swinging up the hill to come at them from opposite sides.

Smitty said, "We could go downhill, while they're split—"

"No future in it," said Brian. "We've got to shoot the horses. It'll be hard to get us out of here then."

114

A few minutes later the Duke's men were rushing them, racing downhill from left and right. The bullets zinged off the rocks and over their heads, fortunately missing them, but they, in turn, hit nothing. As they half rose to fire at the retiring horsemen, the bullets filled the air around them like angry bees.

"They're uphill of us!" shouted young Schmidt, and Brian saw the trick that almost finished them. A few of the Duke's men were armed with semi-automatic weapons, and two of these men had dropped off uphill when the charge started. There they'd waited for their opponents to turn their backs, and only good luck had saved Brian and the others. And now, the siege began.

The sun glared down as the Duke's men crept from cover to cover, a few of them always on horseback, ready to rush in if the chance presented itself. The enemy's ammunition seemed inexhaustible. Young Barnaby got a bullet through the arm. Sharp fragments or rocks brought the blood streaming from Smitty's forehead. Schmidt, crazed by thirst as the afternoon wore on, rose up screaming at the Duke's men, and a steel-jacketed bullet went in one cheek and out the other, leaving him suddenly sober and glaringly conscious that the next piece of insanity would be his last. Brian, deaf from the incessant gunfire, was still unhurt, but aware of his dwindling stock of ammunition and of a growing sense of detachment from reality. The afternoon slid by, and the white sun blazed down from a declining angle. The Duke's men began to work around to take advantage of that angle, knowing that just at sunset, Brian and others would be blinded from that direction.

Brian, roasted by the still-hot sun, his throat parched, lay in the waves of heat reflected from the rocks, and breathed in the odor of gunsmoke and hot horseflesh. He counted his ammunition again. He had three clips left. That was fifteen rounds, plus two shots in his gun. He thought he'd done well to have that much left. But it wasn't going to be enough. And the enemy's ammunition seemed endless.

Somewhere through the heat and the ringing in his ears came a distant wail. The Duke's men pointed, and those more distant squirmed away from the fight and ran to get their horses.

Brian twisted to look out between two rocks.

Down the mountainside, a locomotive thundered around the bend, drawing three freight cars. Atop the front engine fluttered an oblong of cloth, its red and white stripes, and white stars against a blue blackground, bringing a sudden lump to Brian's throat.

Then the Duke's men were racing on horseback toward the engine, waving their guns and firing warning shots. The train slowed, came to a stop. The whine of a bullet over Brian's head warned him that some of the Duke's men were still on hand to keep Brian and the others pinned down. Brian crouched lower, determined to do what he could for the helpless train.

To his astonishment, several of the Duke's men lifted in their saddles, twisted and fell. A machine-gun rattle drifted up from the train.

The remaining horsemen returned the fire.

The sides of the freight cars slammed up and in. There was one concerted motion, and mounted cavalrymen were beside the train. The remainder of the Duke's men fell from their horses, and now the cavalry came up the hill, in two wide arcs, and the pair of the Duke's men who had stayed to pin Brian and the others down were on their feet and running. Brian, Smitty and the two farm boys saw one of their tormentors fall, and the other one stagger, then throw up his hands as suddenly the cavalrymen caught up. Then the cavalry turned and rode to where Brian and the others stood up, swaying with exhaustion and still clutching their guns. The leader of the cavalry, a thin dark man with captain's bars and "U.S." at his lapel, said something to Brian.

Brian heard a faint sound, but pointed to the guns, the rocks, and his deafened ears. The captain spoke again, louder.

"Where are you from? The Duchy?"

Brian nodded, tried to speak, and couldn't. He saw the world begin to sway, and reached out to steady himself against a boulder. The captain turned to one of his men, who dismounted and gave Brian a drink from his canteen.

"You were," said the captain, his face expressionless, "in the Duke's service?"

Brian didn't move, studying the captain's expressionless face. He tried his voice, and the captain said, "Just nod for 'yes.'"

"We were prisoners," said Brian hoarsely. "These two boys were forced labor on a farm. My friend and I were at the Duke's headquarters under guard."

"Doing what?"

"Whatever the Duke told us. We did it or we died of thirst."

"What did he tell you to do?"

"Repair steam engines and steam cars, armor them, work on signals systems and factory repair."

"How long were you there?"

"Since last spring."

"And this was your first chance to escape?"

"We tried once before and didn't make it."

The captain studied them. "Raise your right hands. Face the flag on the locomotive. Repeat after me. 'Before God, I swear allegiance to the flag—'"

Brian and the others steadily repeated the words.

When the oath was completed, the captain relaxed and took out a small leatherbound book, and said, "Names?"

Brian said, "Brian Philips."

Smitty and the others gave their names, then the captain blinked. "Brian Philips," he murmured, flipped back through the book, and said, "Lieutenant, take charge of the burial and prisoner-interrogation details. Stay alert and in view of the lookout station. Troopers Quincy and Howe, dismount and help these two gentlemen into the saddle. All right, Mr. Philips, you and Mr. Smith follow me."

Brian, with no idea what was happening, barely able to cling to the saddle, was rushed to the train and he and Smitty put aboard. The captain called to the trainmen. With a clank of couplings, the train began to back. It reached the base of the embankment below the tall tower

Brian had seen from a distance. The captain sprang from the locomotive to a ladder up the bank, climbing a ladder up the heavy timbers and vanished into the tower. At its peak, big semaphore arms swung up to attention, dropped wide, then swung up again. Then the tower was out of sight as the locomotive backed around a curve onto a track connecting at an angle, dropped off the two rear cars, pulled forward on a second track that curved to rejoin the line they'd been on originally, and then backed up again to the ladder. A few minutes later the captain climbed down and shouted, "Take them all the way to Butte! We'll clear the track in front of you!"

The engineer waved his hand and the train began to move.

A trainman climbed back, heaved on the lever that slammed the long side door shut, then gave each several drinks from a canteen. Brian and Smitty, exhausted, found a pile of loose hay in a wooden pen, sank down in it and immediately were sound asleep.

A loud wailing blast, repeated again and again, woke Brian up sometime after dark. From somewhere far ahead, the blast was answered in kind, a distant wail that was repeated over and over. The engine picked up speed, the heavy *chuffs* becoming faster and faster, weaving a rhythmic pattern that sent Brian off to sleep again. When he next woke up, the engine was silent, and men were shining the beam of acetylene hand-lamps around the car.

Still half awake, Brian was rushed out into a street lit by widely spaced, soft gaslights, into a big building that trembled continuously underfoot. From somewhere came the scream and grind of machinery, then they went through a huge room where piles of coal glistened in the dim light. They passed a door from behind which came a clang and scrape of metal, walked along beside huge, asbestos-wrapped steam pipes, and then again were in a hallway, then rattling up in an elevator to a hall, high up in the building. Here the tremble and shake was less pronounced, the throb of coal-fed steam power just a murmur in the background, and one of the guards was knocking at a door lettered: "James Cardan, President."

"Come in," said the musical voice of Cardan's reception-ist, Barbara Bowen.

Brian looked at her as in a dream, saw her smile, heard her say, "The chief's waiting," and a moment later saw the familiar broad, rugged figure behind the desk. The guards left, and Brian was abruptly wide-awake. He glanced around. Smitty was gone. A cigar rested in a tray on Cardan's desk, a thin wisp of smoke climbing up in the lamplight.

Cardan eyed Brian in silence for a moment. "What kept you from leaving with the rest of us?"

"A crack on the head."

Cardan's eyes seemed to drill into his, boring, seeking, probing. It occurred to Brian that he might not be believed. Suddenly angry, Brian glared back.

Cardan, his voice without intonation, said, "That's the story you told before."

"It's a story I'll never tell a third time."

Cardan looked at him a long moment, searching out his meaning, then suddenly he began to smile. He picked up the cigar, grinned, drew on it, and blew out a long puff of smoke.

"How did it happen this time?"

Brian described it.

Cardan shook his head.

"What happened then? What did you do?"

Brian told him the whole story. Before it was over, Cardan had gotten out a map and was checking the location of the Duke's installations. By the time they'd finished, the sky was growing light in the east, and Cardan said, "I guess it's time I gave *you* some information now."

He drew a rough outline map of the North American continent, penciled in several small ovals along the Eastern Seaboard, and marked the rest of the coastal area with heavy black strokes.

"The heavily settled places are gone—starvation, riots, epidemics, chaos. There are just a few enclaves here and there that held out. Canada came through pretty well, though Quebec split off on its own—it's New France now. The central part of the U.S., we don't know much about, but there's talk of a seaborne expedition through the Panama Canal—which we still hold—and up the Mississippi to find out."

Cardan drew several large ovals. "To the south, there's a colored state called 'Freedom Land,' and a lopsided Texas sandwiched between the 'Apache Nation' and a sort of bandit empire called 'Herrero's Kingdom.' Further north, taking in parts of half a dozen Western and Middlewestern states, we have this damned Duchy. It blocks us off the others. It threatens to lock us up west of the Rockies. When I say 'us,' I mean what nearly everyone calls 'America.' That's Montana, Idaho, Washington, Oregon, large parts of the six adjoining states, and a section of Colorado." He glanced at Brian. "You want to hear this?"

Brian nodded. He had a vague feeling of letdown now that he was finally here, but there was a sense of grim satisfaction, too. He said curiously, "Do we know anything about the rest of the world?"

"Quite a bit. A lot of ocean vessels are steam powered, and armed steamships can travel comparatively unharmed by the loss of electricity. We sent an expedition to try to reach the source of all the trouble, in Afghanistan. They crossed the oceans. But they weren't able to make it all the way."

"Why not?"

"It's not very nice there. Starting at about one hundred eighty miles from the site of the Helmand laboratory, metal becomes increasingly brittle. At about one hundred fifty miles, metal cracks and shatters, and the same effect becomes noticeable with other materials. A heavy leather belt, for instance, can be snapped between the fingers. At around one hundred twenty miles, the same weaknesses noticeably affect the human body. A stumble can mean a broken leg. The bones are brittle. The hands and feet become numb, as if from cold, thought is slow, and the release of energy by the chemistry of the body is slower yet. At a hundred miles, there's a sort of desert. Vegetation is dead or stunted. There's bare dirty sand, and crumbling rocks. The body has become exceptionally fragile, fatigue is continuous and breathing is very difficult—apparently because the body just can't assimilate the oxygen.

All these difficulties seem traceable ultimately to a closer binding of electrons. If this effect extends all the way to the Helmand laboratory itself, it's hard to see why the lab hasn't been destroyed by it. Maclane thinks there may be a belt of interference around the lab, in which the effects are less severe than they are further away. We don't know. But distance makes a difference, and if you'll look on the opposite side of the globe from Afghanistan, you'll find a stretch of the South Pacific containing, among other little bits of real estate, Easter Island. This is about as far away from the Helmand project as you can get on Earth. There, electricity still works. America has taken those islands and heavily fortified them. Quite a few of our men are there. The hope is that we can work out a missile capable of traveling a large part of its flight without benefit of electrical devices, and land it on the Helmand lab. But it's quite a problem."

There was a soft bonging noise, a rattle of wires, and a cylindrical capsule about six inches long and two and a half in diameter traveled along a track and came to rest back of Cardan's desk. He reached out, flipped it open, and sat back to very carefully look through several typewritten sheets of paper. He wrote rapidly on a note pad, tore off the top sheet, folded it in the little capsule, and started it on its way back along the track.

"Donovan and Maclane," said Cardan, "have been grilling Smitty. He tells substantially the same story you do. With this 'Duke,' we have to be careful." Cardan put his cigar in the tray and leaned back, his hands clasped behind his neck. He blew out a cloud of smoke.

"I can offer you a job here or on Easter Island. They need another chemist out there. We need one here. The salary there is higher. But—" He smiled. "—There are other compensations here."

He got up, opened the door to the next room, and spoke quietly to Miss Bowen. He came back, sat down, and knocked the ash off the cigar.

A few minutes later, the door opened.

"Excuse me," said Cardan, getting up. "I have something to say to Miss Bowen."

Brian turned around. Standing in the doorway, her blond hair shining in the early morning sunlight slanting through the window, her blue eyes smiling, stood Anne Cermak.

Brian stood up, looking deep into her clear smiling eyes. Then the eyes changed.

"Oh, Brian," she said, and abruptly he was holding her close.

Long moments later, she said, "Let me—let me show you around the building. We can't stay here like this. Come on." She took his hand, and then Brian was looking at ingenious devices being developed to substitute for electricity. There were miniature steam engines and turbines, flexible insulated lines for conveying steam from central boilers, oil lamps with improved mantles that gave a white clear light and refused to break, unlike the usual fragile mantles. A little device to partially replace the flashlight drew a multitude of flints across a rough steel surface, the many sparks creating a pale white light that an eager technician had Brian try out in a nearby darkroom. There were mechancial phonographs brought to a high state of refinement, and signal system that relied on fluctuations of hydraulic pressure in a long thin tube. To his astonishment, Brian saw substitutes for nearly every one of the simpler electrical devices he was used to. But the very number of the substitutes, and the ingenuity that had had to go into them, showed what a pillar of civilization electricity had been.

"It's fine," he said when they were in Anne's small lab at last, "but it will be a lot better if we can get electricity to work again."

Anne nodded, then smiled suddenly. "We've forgotten something. Dad's on the railroad here, and he's off duty tonight."

Brian looked puzzled.

She laughed. "Don't you remember our dinner date?"

"Oh," he said, smiling. "Am I still invited?"

"Just try to get out of it."

"Well—" He'd forgotten that invitation made what seemed like years ago, just before the electricity went off and Carl came in to tell them Cardan wanted to see them—

And then Brian remembered other things.

"Carl. Where is he?"

"Carl? Why, he has a job here. He used to be on this floor, but Mr. Cardan moved him. I don't know just where—"

"Excuse me a minute." Brian's fists tingled. He was thinking of that last crack on the head, of all the insults and underhanded blows he'd experienced from Carl. He was remembering the difference between Carl and himself. As Carl had said, that difference was that Carl always won. The room around Brian seemed to grow momentarily lighter, then darker. Then his emotions were wrapped in cotton wool, and everything else in his life was put away to wait until he had a chance to settle with Carl.

He went down the hall to Cardan's office. "I'm looking for Carl," he said.

"You're just in time." Cardan turned to the window. "If you're quick enough, you might just manage to see him."

Brian threw the window up and looked out.

Down far below was the open platform of the train station. A long passenger train was starting to move, and just springing aboard was a tall, blond, athletic figure, the suitcase gripped in one hand showing bits of hastily packed shirts sticking out.

Brian studied the distance to the ground. The train gathered speed. It was obvious insanity to try to make the jump to the ground and run a race with a steam locomotive capable of seventy or eighty miles an hour.

But it took a distinct effort for Brian to pull his head back in the window.

"That train is headed for the coast," Cardan told him. "Carl just volunteered for the trip to Easter Island. All I did was tell him you were back."

Brian drew a deep breath, and Cardan watched him

smiling. Cardan had watched the struggle, and he knew what actuated the two men. And Carl's philosophy that he must always win was no defense against someone who always did his best, once that best reached a certain level.

Brian could feel himself gradually readjust to the situation.

If Carl had stayed there, Brian would have had no choice. But now Carl was gone. Brian gradually relaxed, and pulled down the window. He looked at Cardan and grinned.

"I have some questions I'd like to ask—about terms of employment."

Cardan sucked on his cigar. His face took on the shrewdly innocent look of a businessman determined to make a profitable arrangement, but who knew that the arrangement had to be truly profitable to both sides if he was to get the best work.

Then Brian was shaking hands, and was on the way down the hall to see Anne Cermak and make arrangements for their long-delayed dinner date.

Brian's body ached, and his skin felt dry and hot from yesterday's sunburn. He was wearing the same clothes in which he'd been chased across two states and spent the afternoon in a rock pile with a Springfield rifle and four dead horses. He'd been ambushed, shot at, driven through ice and smoke, forced to pillage for his food, turned into a steam-engine rebuilder by endless drudgery, and had only narrowly escaped the job of assistant dictator in one of the cleverest tyrannies since Nazi Germany. It came to Brian that he was a wreck, a shambles, and no woman would want him.

He pushed open the lab door. Anne smiled up at him and came into his arms.

It had been a rough two thousand miles, but at last he'd made it.

Brian was home.

The End

The World Trembled In The Grip
Of A Strange And Horrible Scourge

THE HAMELIN PLAGUE

By A. Bertram Chandler

A MONARCH SCIENCE-FICTION NOVEL

It began with a few small items in the newspapers—dead dogs and cats, a mutilated child, a series of unexplained fires. Then, suddenly, it exploded into a full-sized catastrophe. Huge mutants—half rat, half man—began taking over the world, destroying whole cities and their populations.

Dr. Piper was the only hope for personal and world survival—if he was still alive—and if the King Rats hadn't forced him to serve their evil purpose.

You'll find top-notch science-fiction reading in this MONARCH book and other outstanding novels such as:

A Gripping Story Of A Man Who
Destroyed Himself To Cure An . . . . .

OBSESSION

By Lionel White

Author of MARILYN K.

A MONARCH SUSPENSE SPECIAL

If Conrad Madden hadn't had a fight with his wife; if he hadn't been irritated by his children; if he hadn't been out of a job for two months; if he hadn't had too much to drink; if he hadn't agreed to take the baby-sitter home that night; if he hadn't succumbed to her throaty-voiced offer to "come up for a nightcap" . . .

He would never have been caught up in a rebellion against his humdrum life, and an OBSESSION over a girl half his age.

Read this thrilling suspense-filled MONARCH BOOK and these other titles available in this new series: